Jumbo Spencer

Also by Helen Cresswell

THE WHITE SEA HORSE

J·B·LIPPINCOTT COMPANY

PHILADELPHIA *and* NEW YORK

1966

JUMBO SPENCER

by Helen Cresswell

Illustrated by VICTORIA de LARREA

For
the twins
Sandra and Shirley

Text copyright © 1963 by Helen Rowe
Illustrations copyright © 1966 by Victoria de Larrea
Library of Congress Catalog Card Number AC 66–10031
FIRST AMERICAN EDITION
First Published by Brockhampton Press Ltd.

TYPOGRAPHY BY TERE LOPRETE

CONTENTS

1

AN IDEA IS BORN

Jumbo Spencer trudged alone up the white, shadowless lane to the village. He was alone because he wished to think.

"You go on ahead," he had ordered the others. "I want to think."

Obediently Maggots, Freckles, and Mike had set off without him. Jumbo had sat on the school fence and watched them go, giving them a good start.

"Don't hang about!" he had shouted after them. "I'm coming in a minute!"

With approval he had seen their steps quicken. He had noticed that Maggots' short brown legs with their white socks were working twice as hard as Freckles' and Mike's.

Poor Maggots, he had thought. Still, that's the penalty of being a girl.

It was quiet now, almost unbearably quiet after the deafening cheers at the breaking up ceremony. Jumbo looked at his watch. It was just noon. The dry grass shimmered in the heat and in the distance he could hear the whirr of a combine harvester.

When he had given them a few minutes' start Jumbo eased himself off the fence and set off up the lane. Occasionally he became aware that the blackbird on the five-barred gate was whistling fit to burst, or that the ten-acre field was molten gold with buttercups, but on the whole he was far too busy thinking to notice.

"This holiday's going to be the best yet," he decided.

This, he realized, was asking a good deal, because every holiday up till now had been such a riotous, care-free, satisfying experience, that to ask for more seemed a little ungrateful, perhaps even greedy.

Take last holiday, for instance. He always thought of that as The Camping Holiday. He and the gang had set up camp in Shoredale Woods on the first day and had stayed there till the day before they went back to school. He was not saying that he would have gone had he known that there were going to be gales and hailstorms practically every day, but looking back he did not regret that experience. He felt it had hardened them up, given them some idea of the sterner side of life.

He had been getting into a rut. What could be more boring, he had argued, than to spend eleven years between four walls with a roof over your head, and knowing that every morning at seven you will be awakened by your mother calling you to breakfast?

His mother had said that most people managed to do it for a lifetime without being bored, let alone eleven years, adding weakly that she didn't know why her son couldn't be like everyone else. It was at this point that Jumbo had known the argument was won.

"That's just it!" he had cried triumphantly. "I'm not like anyone else. That's the whole point. And I don't want to be, either. I'm bored with living between four walls!"

With a shock Jumbo found himself at the top of the High Street.

Goodness! he thought with disgust. Here I am already. I've just wasted that walk.

He saw the others waiting for him by the Pump, spread-eagled on the grass like starfish. He could see the scarlet of Maggots' skirt brilliantly displayed on the green. He slowed his pace, playing for time. He knew they were waiting to hear the outcome of his mile-long "think" from the school. He had to tell them something.

"Hullo," he said casually, as if he had not been expecting to see them. "It's hot."

"I know," said Maggots. "It's dripping off me. Oh, Jumbo, have you thought of something?"

Trust a girl! thought Jumbo bitterly. Trust a girl to come straight at you like that, like a sock on the jaw!

With boys he could have steered round it, used a bit

of diplomacy. He eyed her sternly and she dropped her gaze.

"Of course," he said.

"Oh, Jumbo!" she cried. "What is it? Oh, do tell us. Sit down, Jumbo!"

She patted the grass beside her invitingly as if she were plumping a cushion.

"No, thanks. Can't stop. I've got something important to do. I'll see you all later."

"The idea, Jumbo! Aren't you going to t-t-tell us it?"

It was Mike, speaking slowly and heavily as though he were mentally spelling every word before he said it. Sometimes he stammered as if there were a word he was not quite sure how to spell.

"Not now," said Jumbo. It would do them good to be kept in suspense. Besides, it would take all afternoon to think of something. "We'll make it after tea. Six o'clock in the barn, right?"

"Right!" they chorused.

"Good. Six o'clock sharp."

He turned and went on up the High Street, walking casually. They must not suspect that he knew no more than they how they were to spend the next seven weeks. He went through the farmyard gate banging it behind him, and made a sudden spurt across the cobbles, sending hens and turkeys squawking in all directions. He was suddenly glad to be home, and that it was the last day of school. The moment he opened the door and went down the stone steps it was cool and shady. He poured a glass of lemonade from the enormous earthenware jug in which his mother made it. She came in.

"Why don't you go for a picnic this afternoon, dear, with your friends? I'll pack you some sandwiches."

Jumbo looked hard at his mother. She was smiling, but he knew what she was thinking.

Trying to get me out of the way already, he thought. Haven't been on holiday half an hour yet, and she's already trying to get me out of the house.

"No," he said out loud, "I don't want to go on a picnic, thank you. I have things on my mind."

"Oh?" His mother stopped in her tracks and took a searching look at him. "Oh, I see."

"After dinner, I'll just go and sit in the orchard while I think things over," said Jumbo. "I can think better out there."

So he could, usually. But it was a hot day, and for dinner he had soup, roast lamb, mint sauce, two kinds of potatoes, and fruit salad and ice-cream. And when he went into the orchard and lay on the silky grass that grew in the shade, it seemed natural to close his eyes, because the leaves above him were hypnotizing him with their waving motion and thousand eyes of green and gold. Then the next thing he heard was his mother's voice calling from a long way off as though he were at the bottom of a deep well:

"Jumbo! Jumbo! It's tea-time!"

He opened his eyes with an effort and was surprised

to see that she was there, standing right over him. He could have sworn she was a million miles away.

The trouble was, thought Jumbo, as he sat down to tea, that very soon they would be asking questions, and he didn't know the answers. It was maddening. Here he was, longing for an idea that would make this holiday the best they had ever known, and not a thing would come. It was lack of inspiration, of course. He had read about it. Poets had it as well.

He realized that his mother was drawing one side of the curtain across the window.

"Oh, not television, Mum!" he cried in agony. "I'm trying to *think!*"

"Still, dear?" she smiled. "Never mind, I only want the news, then we'll have it off."

Jumbo groaned. It was six o'clock. The gang would already be waiting for him in the barn, and here he sat with the television going full blare and not a single idea in his head. All he could see was the sun shining across his plate like a warning finger, and a fly buzzing round the honey pot, round and round and round in angry, pointless little circles.

Through his trance the voice of the news announcer came like a voice from another world:

". . . and above all, he was a great reformer and a leader of men."

There was silence. The curtains swished and the sun came flooding back into the room.

"I've heard the headlines, that's enough," said his mother. Jumbo hardly heard her. Running through his brain in a kind of refrain, almost like poetry, were the words he had just heard. "He was a great reformer and a leader of men."

"Mum?"

"Yes, dear?"

"What's a reformer?"

"Oh, a man who tries to put things right. You mean the man they were just talking about? Yes, he was a great social reformer. A lot of people must be grateful to him."

"What kinds of things did he put right?" pressed Jumbo.

"All kinds of things," said his mother vaguely. "He was always putting things right and making life better for people."

"A great reformer and a leader of men!" Jumbo felt almost bursting. That was it! That's what he was! He'd always known it, but had never really known the words. He was the leader of Freckles, Maggots, and Mike! A leader of men! He put down his knife and made blindly for the door.

"Where are you going?" cried his mother. "You haven't drunk your tea!"

But Jumbo did not hear her. He was racing down the hill, his arms whirling like windmills, with the words "a great reformer and a leader of men" ringing like music in his ears over and over again.

2

THE JUMBO SPENCER REFORM CLUB

Jumbo Spencer raced down the hill with a head full of glory and skidded to a halt outside the barn. Here he stopped and arranged himself to make an entrance. It mustn't look as if he had been running because he was late. He hadn't, anyway.

On the door was a notice printed in red and orange. It said: THE JUMBO SPENCER MEMORIAL THEATRE. Plays produced and directed by Jumbo Spencer. Admission 6d.

Jumbo tore down the notice with a single sweeping movement. He stood trying to think of a suitable one to replace it, but nothing came. He hadn't had the idea long enough yet to be shooting off inspirations like leaves. He would take care of everything in good time.

He entered the shadowy barn, finding it hard to conceal his excitement beneath the calm, controlled exterior

suitable for a leader of men. When he reached the end of the barn he mounted his wooden platform and looked down on the upturned faces of his friends.

The homely, admiring face of Mike, Freckles' quick-silver features, and Maggots' face shining with joy, all seemed to have taken on a new meaning. Jumbo looked down on them and thought solemnly, These are my men. I am a leader, and these are the men I must lead.

The thought touched him so much that he could hardly speak, and they continued to gaze up at him, waiting. They were in his hands, and realizing this he felt an upsurge of pride and power.

"Well, men," he said, using the term unconsciously, although they looked a little startled. "I expect you are waiting to hear the idea."

The two boys nodded and Maggots burst out with an excited, "Oh, yes, please, Jumbo!"

"It's a new idea," went on Jumbo. "It's such a new idea that at first you are going to be surprised. But there isn't the slightest doubt that it's the best idea I've ever had. I have ever had," he repeated.

"What we are going to do these holidays," he said, "is reform the village of Shoredale."

He paused and watched to see what effect his words were having. The reactions of his followers were dis-appointing. Freckles was scratching his head and just stopped himself in time from pulling a face at Mike. Mike sat there unashamedly gaping, his eyes fixed on Jumbo in sheer bewilderment and respect. Maggots gave a little gasp and cried, "Ooooh, Jumbo! What's that?"

"I'm just going to explain," said Jumbo reprovingly, and Mike's features relaxed. He hadn't liked to ask, but he didn't know what Jumbo was talking about, either.

"From time to time," said Jumbo, sticking his thumbs into his braces, "there have been in history great reformers and leaders of men. Great reformers and leaders of men." He repeated the words. He just couldn't help it. They were so beautiful, and at that moment were the only really firm thought he had in his head.

"I believe," said Jumbo modestly, "that I am one of these men."

Maggots gave a little gasp and her hand flew to her mouth.

"I intend to reform the village of Shoredale," Jumbo went on. "I intend to reform it until its own grandmother wouldn't recognize it. I intend to sweep it clean of vice and poverty, to turn out the darkest corners and let in the light."

He felt his words building up into a rhythm just like that of the politicians on television, and found himself wondering wherever he had found such beautiful ideas.

"Jumbo . . ." said Maggots falteringly.

"What is it?" asked Jumbo quite kindly.

"I think I see what you mean about sweeping the streets, but I'm only ten." Her face flushed dark red but she struggled on, "And, Jumbo, I don't think I *really* quite know what reforming is."

Jumbo paused. He paused for a long time as if emotion prevented him from speaking, and when he spoke again it was quietly and sadly.

"I was afraid not," he said. "To reform, Maggots, means to make things better. To make all kinds of things better for people."

He made a vague gesture with his hands.

"What kind of things, Jumbo?" asked Maggots. Her face was alight with interest now.

He might have known that she wouldn't be content just with the spirit of the thing, but would start asking all kinds of awkward questions that he hadn't yet had time to find the answers to.

"It's the spirit of the thing!" he cried. "Can't girls ever get the spirit of a thing? You get it, don't you, Mike? And you, Freckles?"

"Oh yes, Jumbo, I g-get it," stammered Mike. At the moment his mind was confused, but somewhere a light was breaking through and he had a vague, pleasant impression that here was something glorious and fine, and he felt sure that it wouldn't be long before he got it altogether.

"You see, Maggots," said Jumbo severely, "the others get it."

She hung her head and he said more kindly:

"Don't worry, Maggots, you will in the end."

"What are we going to reform, Jumbo?" asked Freckles, the idea just striking him.

"We'll have to get to grips with that," Jumbo told him. He had noticed how fond politicians were of get-

ting to grips with things. "We had better make out a
list of all the things that are wrong with Shoredale.
Then we can set about putting them right."

He folded his arms impressed with his own logic.
Freckles immediately produced a pad and pencil and
offered it to him.

"Here you are, Jumbo."

He took it, feeling that he had his back to the wall
again. Being a leader of men wasn't easy, he decided.
There was a silence.

"Suggestions?" said Jumbo.

The barn was shadowy and still with thought.

"We could do with a cinema?" suggested Freckles at
last.

"Freckles," said Jumbo, "we are *reforming* Shoredale, not turning it into a pleasure park. We have to do
things that make people's lives better. We have to right
wrongs."

"My mother says it's a crying shame we haven't got
a cinema," muttered Freckles rebelliously. This Jumbo
ignored.

There was another desperate silence, when Jumbo,
tired of inaction, broke out:

"I'll tell you what, we could have a census. You
know, go round to people's houses and ask them ques-
tions. Ask them what they thought was wrong with
Shoredale. That's what we'll do. We'll do it tomorrow.
We'll do all kinds of things. Three cheers for the Jumbo
Spencer Reform Club. Hip hip—"

"Hooray!" yelled the other three, getting up and dancing about, sure that with Jumbo in this mood the meeting was now over.

"Come on!" yelled Jumbo, leaping down from his platform. "Let's go and take a look at the village. It might give us some ideas."

They raced out, slamming the door behind them. The cows in the field looked faintly surprised but not altogether baffled, because Jumbo was well known to them.

It was a beautiful evening and when they reached the top of the hill they could see the village lying in a great calm pool of golden light. It looked all right to Jumbo. You wouldn't think there was a thing wrong with it, he thought. But that was the trouble, you could never tell just by looking at things. And whatever was wrong with Shoredale, he, Jumbo Spencer, was going to put right. He could feel the heady, exciting words beginning to run through his brain again: "A great reformer and a leader of men."

"Come on men!" he shouted. "Let's go!"

And Jumbo Spencer, social reformer and leader of men, set off down the hill with his faithful followers strung out behind him like the tail of a soaring kite. The battle had begun.

3

JUMBO HOLDS
A CENSUS

It took several days for the Jumbo Spencer Reform Club to get under way. For the first two days Jumbo shut himself up in his room or lay in the orchard reading some books Freckles had fetched him from the library. When he finally emerged he felt a good deal wiser and better fitted to be a leader of men. He came down at tea-time on the second day. His mother looked hard at him.

"Jumbo," she said, "what's that you're wearing?"

It was a bow tie. His father's bow tie, to be exact. In all the photographs Jumbo had seen in the books he was reading, at least half the men were wearing them. He thought he knew why. The moment he had put it on and seen his reflection in the glass he had felt wiser and more experienced.

"I'm sick of wearing a tie," he said. "It's boring, wearing one all the time. I like to be different."

"Well, you certainly look different in that. And when your father sees you, you'll probably feel different!"

"I only borrowed this one until I get one of my own," said Jumbo. "I shall get several, so that it doesn't get boring for people always seeing me in the same one."

"Are you going out tonight?" asked his mother. "You've been in the house long enough. It's time you got some fresh air."

There she goes again, thought Jumbo wearily. She was always trying to get him out of the house, as if he were a cockroach or something. He'd been so quiet she could hardly have known he was there.

"As a matter of fact I am," he said, "not for the fresh air, though. I'm going down to address the club."

"I see." His mother turned away and Jumbo was perfectly aware that she was hiding a smile. He didn't mind. He had gathered from his reading that social reformers were always made fun of by people who didn't understand them.

"I'd better be going," he said, "the men will be waiting."

In any case, his father would be in from the fields at any time and Jumbo didn't really want to run into him wearing his bow tie.

Unfortunately, there was a little clump of boys at the top of the High Street who giggled and pointed at him and tapped their fingers rudely against their foreheads when they saw his bow tie, but Jumbo marched loftily past them. Normally he would have stopped, grabbed two of them and cracked their heads together, but he felt that to do this would be unbecoming to his new position.

Freckles, Mike, and Maggots boggled gratifyingly at his bow tie, but not one of them said anything. This pleased him, because it showed that they realized that he was somehow different from other people and had a right to dress as if he were.

"Well," he said, "are you all ready for the census? Got your notebooks and pencils?"

They all nodded.

"Right. I'll start on this side of the road at the bottom and work up. Mike, you start on the other side of the road, and, Freckles, you take Top Lane and Shepherd's Lane. Maggots, you can come with me."

He didn't want Maggots asking questions. In any case, she would probably giggle and give the wrong impression.

He walked with determination to the end house on the High Street. He knocked and then turned to look sternly at Maggots.

"No giggling, now," he said.

The door opened. It was Mr. Jefferson, the butcher, with his hair on end and his tie half on. He was just getting ready to go out.

"Good evening, Mr. Jefferson," said Jumbo politely.

"I'm Jumbo Spencer and I would like to ask you a few questions."

"I haven't lived in this village all these years without knowing perfectly well who you are, young Spencer," said Mr. Jefferson rudely. "And to save you the trouble of asking, no, I don't want any tickets for the Spencer Memorial Theatre, and no, I don't want any jobs doing, and no, Bob can't come out—he's going out with his mother and me. Does that answer your questions?"

Jumbo stood his ground. He had been prepared for this.

"No, sir," he said politely. "I wanted to ask you what you think is wrong with Shoredale?"

"To *what?*" almost roared the butcher. "You want to ask me what's wrong with Shoredale? Well, I'll tell you. The trouble with Shoredale is that you can't have five minutes' peace and quiet in your own house without some idiot coming banging on your door asking stupid questions. That's what's wrong!"

"This is a serious question, Mr. Jefferson," said Jumbo. "I really want to know your opinion."

"That *is* my opinion!" yelled Mr. Jefferson, "and you're welcome to it!"

The door banged shut.

"Oh, Jumbo," whispered Maggots, "wasn't he rude to you!"

Jumbo glanced sideways and saw that her eyes were brimming with tears. It warmed him somehow, and made him feel strong and great.

"Never mind, Maggots," he said. "You always get people like that."

All the same, instead of taking the next house he turned back and walked in the direction of the church. He rather liked the vicar, and at least he didn't shout at people.

Jumbo took his time because he enjoyed walking up the lane and through the churchyard. He clasped his hands behind his back and scrunched steadily forward up the gravel path. The rectory was covered with a glinting coat of ivy. It was just right for the vicar, he decided. He was a nice man, and deserved to live in a house overlooking a graveyard. He doubted whether much reforming would be needed here, but at least he might get some ideas.

The door was opened by Mr. Potter himself.

"Ah, good evening, Spencer," he said. "Hello, Maggie."

"Good evening, Mr. Potter," said Jumbo pleasantly. "I hope I haven't interrupted the writing of your sermon?"

"Oh, not at all, not at all. What can I do for you?"

"It was just a few questions that I wanted to ask you," explained Jumbo.

"Of course," said Mr. Potter, puzzled but patient. "Fire away."

"They're not usual kind of questions," said Jumbo. "They're about reform. You see, I have formed a club, the Jumbo Spencer Reform Club, and this holiday we're going to reform Shoredale."

"Ah, I see." Mr. Potter tried very hard to keep his eyes off Jumbo's bow tie. "That's very interesting, Spencer. Very interesting indeed. And I wish you every success. It's something I've been trying to do myself for some years now. Nearly twenty years, in fact. Perhaps you may be able to help *me?*"

"Oh I hope so, sir," said Jumbo modestly. "That's what I thought. We could kind of exchange ideas. I wondered what you thought needed reforming?"

The vicar hesitated for a moment.

"Now, let me see," he said. "Had you thought of including yourself and your friends in this reform?"

"Oh yes," said Jumbo. "Definitely. We realize that we need it as much as anyone."

"Good, good. That's half the battle then. Now, let's see. It's Sunday tomorrow, isn't it?"

"Yes, sir."

"Well, might I suggest that you and your friends get the club off to a flying start by coming to church tomorrow morning?"

Jumbo did not bat an eyelid.

"We will, definitely," he said. "All of us."

Mr. Potter looked somewhat taken aback, as Jumbo had known he would.

"Anything else?" asked Jumbo.

"Well, of course, there's the little matter of a village

hall, for a youth club, and so on," he said playfully.

"So there is!" cried Jumbo joyfully. "Of course, I'd forgotten that. And a playing-field, too. Thank you, Mr. Potter. Maggots, make a note of it. You've been a great help, Mr. Potter. Thank you very much. Come on, Maggots."

"Good-bye, good-bye!" he called after them.

"See you in church!" called Jumbo over his shoulder.

By seven o'clock he had covered his side of the High Street and had all kinds of suggestions. Some of them were unkind, but others he thought were quite useful. For instance, old Miss Mogg had suggested a zebra crossing from her gate to the post office, and Jumbo thought that this could easily be arranged. Mrs. Baker thought the trees and shrubs in the High Street and churchyard were untidy and needed clipping, and this, too, Jumbo felt equal to deal with.

They reported in turn while Jumbo listened intently. He made a note of some useful suggestions such as a baby-sitting service, and there were several suggestions that there should be a village youth club—mainly to keep Jumbo and his friends off the streets.

"That's definitely one of the things we must have," said Jumbo. "And a playing-field. Mr. Potter agrees with me."

"Mr. P-p-p-potter?" said Mike. "Have you been to see the v-v-vicar, Jumbo?"

"Yes, I have," said Jumbo, "and that reminds me. You're to go to church tomorrow, all of you. We'll meet by the lich-gate at ten to eleven, and mind you look tidy. We want to make a good impression."

"Oh, Jumbo," said Mike, "n-n-need we?"

"Yes," said Jumbo, "we need. Maggots, can you sew?"

"Oh, yes!" said Maggots.

"Good. Then you can make me some bow ties, like the one I'm wearing. I've got another here you can copy. I'd like one for tomorrow, if you can manage it."

"Oh yes, Jumbo," said Maggots gladly.

"Good. Mike, your father's got plenty of paint, hasn't he? I want you to bring a tin of black and a tin of white and some brushes down to the barn tomorrow. And all of you bring all the hedge clippers and pruning shears you can lay your hands on as well."

"It's going to be hard work," said Freckles gloomily.

Jumbo regarded him severely.

"Reform *is* hard work," he said. "It doesn't grow on trees. In any case, I can probably organize someone else to do the actual work. It's the brain work that counts in a thing like this. The hardest part is making the decisions."

"Jumbo," said Maggots, "I've been thinking. I can see how it might be easy to do some things, but, Jumbo, how are we going to get a village hall?"

Again Jumbo realized how awkward it was to have a girl in the outfit. He racked his brains to think of things he had read and heard. The thing that seemed to stand out most was a newsreel he had seen lately about a "Ban the Bomb" march, with a procession of people nearly a mile long, all carrying banners and shouting slogans. The idea fired him.

"That's easy. Who's the richest man in this village?"

"Mr. Bennett!" they chorused.

"Exactly," nodded Jumbo. "He could pay for a hall a hundred times over if he wanted to. So we'll take a petition to him. And if that fails," he paused so that his next words would have the maximum effect, "if that fails, we'll have a march!"

"A march!" breathed Maggots. "Oh, Jumbo!"

"We'll all march up there to his house and refuse to move," said Jumbo, the idea beginning to take shape. "We can take blankets and food and portable radios and plenty to eat, and just stay there until he gives in. We can cook sausages on an oil stove. We might even get it filmed on television and the whole country would be up in arms. He'd have to give in."

"Oh, yes!" cried Maggots. "He would, Jumbo, he would! Oh, you do have marvellous ideas!"

"We'll deal with that later, though," said Jumbo. "Now I'll see you all at the lich-gate at ten to eleven. Mike, you'd better bring Towser to guard the tools while we're in there."

Towser was Mike's large, ferocious-looking boxer with teeth like piano keys.

"But, Jumbo, Towser doesn't like m-music," protested Mike. "He'll howl."

"Let him," said Jumbo. "We can sing louder than he can howl, can't we?"

He walked off up the High Street. People stared at his bow tie and he walked slowly so that they could get a good look at it. When he got home his father was having supper.

"Hello, son," he said.

"Hello, Dad," said Jumbo. "I'm off to bed now, I'm tired."

"Just a minute," said his father. "Is that my bow tie you've got on?"

"Yes, Dad," said Jumbo.

"What for? Memorial Theatre opened up again?"

"No, Dad, I'm always going to wear a bow tie."

"You're *what?*"

"Always going to wear one. You'll get used to it, Dad. I'll put this one back as I go up. Good night."

As he went up he could hear his father calling his mother, and he smiled. She would explain about his being a reformer and leader of men better than he could.

He'd done a day's work.

4

THE FIRST BLOW
IS STRUCK

Sunday was on the whole a quiet day. Jumbo never intended it to be anything else. He had respect for Sunday. Whatever anybody said it was somehow different from any other day of the week. The moment you opened your eyes you knew it was Sunday. The fields were quieter, almost at rest, and the streets were silent. He liked it, and meant to keep it that way. It gave him time to think. Jumbo believed that any plan needed a good deal of spade-work in the way of thinking before it could be a success.

By nine o'clock Maggots had called with Jumbo's bow tie and by ten to eleven Jumbo was at the lich-gate to inspect the gang. They wore their best suits, their hair was wet and plastered well down, their shoes shone, and Jumbo felt that they did him credit. Maggots looked quite nice for a girl, with her blue silk dress, straw hat, and white shoes and socks.

Mike had Towser with him, straining ferociously at the end of the chain. The good thing about Towser was that everyone thought he would eat you as soon as look at you, whereas the truth was that he would run a mile if you so much as snapped your fingers at him. Mike wound his chain carefully round the iron railings and put the heap of paint pots, brushes, and tools next to him.

"Guard, Towser," he said. The boxer obligingly sat on the two nearest paint brushes and bared his teeth horrifyingly.

"That's good," said Jumbo. "Hold it like that, Towser."

They set off up the path to the church. A group of the older village girls and boys stood in the porch, and they nudged each other and grinned. Jumbo heard several remarks about his polka-dot bow tie, but managed to look as if he hadn't.

During the service Jumbo and his friends sang very loudly. They felt they owed it to Mr. Potter, because they had left Towser chained to the railings knowing full well that he would howl as soon as the organ began to play. And when Jumbo and the rest sang loudly, the other village gangs, not to be outdone, sang loudly, too, and the result was very cheerful singing, and you could see that Mr. Potter was pleased with his hymns that Sunday.

When they came out, the other gangs followed them, hanging round the lich-gate to see what Jumbo would do next.

"Look at Laurence Olivier!" yelled Bert Stiggins, leader of a rival gang. "Doesn't half fancy himself in his bow tie!"

Jumbo gazed placidly into the distance over the gold meadows and felt pleasantly above such things. He and his gang gathered up their belongings, released Towser, and set off to the barn.

There Jumbo gave his men a short talk about reform from a book he had just finished, and gave them enough jobs to keep them busy for the rest of the day.

Mike he took on one side and carefully gave him some instructions. It took several minutes to impress on Mike exactly what he wanted him to do, and when he had finished Jumbo made him repeat it back to him, to make sure he had got it right.

Then he went up alone into the village looking for trouble. He found it waiting for him by the Pump, in the shape of Bert Stiggins and his gang.

He walked straight up to them.

"Hello, Bert," he said.

"Hello," said Bert, his eyes fixed rudely and obviously on his bow tie. "I like your pretty little bow. We all do, don't we, chaps?"

The rest of the gang sniggered.

"I'm glad," said Jumbo pleasantly.

"What's it all about, then?" asked Bert.

"All what?" asked Jumbo innocently.

"All this wearing bow ties and going to church and carrying pots of paint round with you," said Bert.

"I can't tell you, Bert," said Jumbo sadly. "I'd like to, but I can't. I will as soon as I can."

"Aw, tell us," said Bert. "We won't laugh, honest. Will we?"

He turned to the gang, who hastily assured him that they would not.

"Laugh?" said Jumbo. "*Laugh?* I should think you wouldn't! No, Bert, I can't say a word. See you at church next Sunday?"

With this he continued up the High Street, certain

that Bert Stiggins' curiosity was roused to fever pitch, and the groundwork for his plan was well laid.

He was right. Bert *was* mystified.

"Well, what do you reckon all that's about, then?" he inquired of the gang in general. "Old Jumbo's up to something, you mark my words. That bow tie means something . . ."

Just then the tall bony figure of Mike appeared at the end of the High Street. Bert's eyes narrowed.

"Look who's coming," he said, "Mike, the Brain of the Century himself. If Jumbo's up to something, he knows about it, and I'm going to get it out of him. Come on!"

He and his gang spread themselves across the High Street blocking Mike's path.

"Hello, Mike," said Bert Stiggins, smiling pleasantly and trying not to lick his lips. "How are things?"

"Very well, thank you, B-B-Bert," stammered Mike.

His expression was glazed and terrified. This pleased Bert, who put it down to a proper respect for his own person. In actual fact, it was due to Mike's frantic effort to remember everything that Jumbo had just told him in the barn. It was over five minutes ago, and was already growing hazy in his mind.

"Quite good, isn't it, Jumbo's latest little scheme?" said Bert winningly.

"What scheme?" said Mike vacantly.

"You know!" said Bert, nudging him in the ribs. "His latest!"

"O-o-o-oh!" said Mike, "you mean the one about cutting the trees and hedges?"

The gang gasped and drew nearer, but Bert frowned warningly at them. Mike's hand was already at his mouth and his face aghast.

"I said I wouldn't tell!" he cried.

"Never mind," said Bert soothingly, "Jumbo'll never know. We won't tell him, will we, chaps? Going to cut what trees and hedges, Mike?"

"I don't know if I ought to tell you," quavered Mike.

"Go on," wheedled Bert, "we won't tell, honest."

"W-well, it's the trees and hedges in the High Street. We're all g-going to get up at s-seven o'clock tomorrow morning and c-c-cut them."

"Cut them *down?*" squeaked Bert incredulously. "Oh lor, he'll be for it!"

"No, not cut them d-d-down," explained Mike, "trim them up, make them look g-good."

"You mean to tell me Jumbo's going to get up at seven o'clock to trim the bushes in the High Street?" almost shrieked Bert. "I don't believe it!"

"Sssssssh!" hissed Mike, looking round. "Someone might hear!"

"Why's he want to trim the hedges?" demanded Bert. "And why's he got to get up at seven o'clock to do it?"

"So that no one else can do it first," said Mike. "That's the whole point. We've got to beat everyone else."

"Who else wants to clip the hedges, for heaven's sake!" exploded the exasperated Bert.

"You never know," said Mike darkly. "We c-can't risk it."

He looked nervously over his shoulder.

"Look, here's Freckles and Maggots. I must go. If they see me talking to you they might tell Jumbo, and he'll know I've spilled the beans. You won't tell, w-will you?" he pleaded.

"Course not," snapped Bert. He watched Mike shamble off up the High Street.

"It's a mystery, that's wot it is," he told the gang. "It don't make sense. Jumbo Spencer getting up at seven o'clock to trim hedges and clip trees."

"Perhaps Mike was pulling our leg?" suggested Dick Perkins.

"Hasn't got the brains," said Bert briefly. "I'll tell you what: let's go down to the barn now while they're all having dinner, and look round."

When they reached the barn Bert crept on ahead to make sure that no one was there.

"Phew! Look at this!" Bert was delving in a corner among the straw. "Hedge clippers. Pruning shears! Mike was telling the truth. Now, what's at the back of it?"

The whole gang sat down and thought hard and long.

"Supposing," said Bert Stiggins at last, "supposing a big event was going to take place in Shoredale next month?"

The rest of the gang looked blank.

"Supposing it was at the church?" prompted Bert.

There was still no response.

"With bells ringing, and confetti all over the place!" yelled Bert desperately.

"A-a-ah!" said Dick Perkins, enlightenment spreading over his face. "You mean Mr. Bennet's granddaughter getting married?"

"Yes," gritted Bert, "that's wot I mean. Bright lot you are to pit your wits against Jumbo Spencer. You couldn't pit them against a circus flea. Now, supposing someone wanted the village to look its best for that day, with important people coming down from London for the wedding, and photos in the newspapers, and all that. Who would that person be? Think hard," he added sarcastically.

"Mr. Bennet?" suggested Dick Perkins at last.

"Mr. Bennet," nodded Bert. "Now, is getting up at seven o'clock to cut hedges the kind of favor you'd expect Jumbo Spencer to do for Mr. Bennet?"

"Oh no, Bert," said Cyril Boot, "not after Mr. Bennet locked him in the shed all night when he was poaching last Easter."

"So wot do you think Jumbo's doing it for?" asked Bert. "Love, or——?"

"Money?" suggested Dick, feeling he was on very good form.

"Money!" said Bert. "That's the answer. Mr. Bennet must have offered some money—five pounds, say—to anyone who tidies up the High Street between now and the wedding. That's why Jumbo's in such a hurry and keeping so quiet about it. He's afraid we'll hear about it and get in first!"

"And we *have* heard about it!" cried Cyril triumphantly.

"And we know wot to do about it," said Bert, a sly smile creeping across his face. "Jumbo Spencer thinks he runs this village, but pretty soon he's going to find out that he's up against a mastermind. A mastermind!"

Jumbo was awakened by the shrilling of his alarm clock. He had stuffed it inside a pair of socks to muffle some of the noise, but it still sounded too piercing to be pleasant at dawn, and he hastily pushed in the button to stop the bell.

The sky was gray and turning to pink, and the dawn chorus was singing lustily. Quietly he opened the window and put his head out, listening. Very faintly, in the distance, he could hear the noise he was expecting. A muffled "clip clip" and an occasional whirr and crash as though a tree were falling. Then he heard a window slam and a man's voice shouting. A smile flitted over his face. Softly he closed the window, tiptoed back to his bed, pulled the still warm clothes over his head, and was asleep again.

The next time he woke it was broad daylight. He went to the window. It was a glorious day. The sun was pitchforking light like straw over the fields and trees. Jumbo felt glad to be alive and a leader of men.

He dressed and went down to the kitchen where the

sun lay in pools on the flagstones and the smell of frying ham and eggs put the final crown of perfection on the day. At five to eight Mike, Freckles, and Maggots were waiting for him by the gate, and at eight o'clock precisely they appeared at the top of the High Street. Everything was perfect.

The High Street was transformed. Every bush was neatly trimmed, the trees had been lopped and the branches swept away. Someone had even mown the grass verge. There was a smell of newly cut leaves, and the bushes cast clear, sharp-edged shadows, like cutouts. By the Pump stood the only untidy things to be seen. It was Bert Stiggins and his gang, and Jumbo could not help feeling that they spoiled the picture.

He saw that Bert was grinning widely—almost helplessly.

"Well, Jumbo?" said Bert as soon as he was within earshot, unable to contain his triumph a second longer.

"Well, Bert!" said Jumbo pleasantly. "I'm surprised to see you about so early."

"Oh, we've been up a long time, ain't we, boys?" smirked Bert. "Since the crack of dawn. How d'ye like the High Street now we've done it?"

"Very nice," said Jumbo warmly. "It looks a picture. I must say, Bert, I've altered my opinion of you. Getting up at five—or was it four—in the morning, to give everyone a nice surprise. Yes, Bert, I think I've misjudged you. I'd like to shake hands, if I may?"

" 'Ere!" Bert backed away suspiciously, eyeing

Jumbo's outstretched hand warily, as if he suspected it of being charged with high voltage electric current. "I don't get this."

Jumbo stood with his hand outstretched while Bert stared at it.

"Aren't you mad, then?" he said.

"Why should I be?" asked Jumbo.

"Well, with us getting in first and doing the clipping, and that."

"Not at all!" said Jumbo heartily. "We were going to do it, but now you've done it, and the job's done. I'm glad, really—we've got quite a full program."

Bert was baffled. Despite everything, Jumbo always seemed to come off best. He was busy searching his mind to frame another question when Jumbo said:

"Well, we've got plenty to do yet. Good-bye, Bert. Jolly good work."

He set off down the High Street followed by Freckles, Mike, and Maggots, all grinning widely.

The first round was over and won. The first reform in Shoredale had taken place. Jumbo stopped and looked back to where the village lay in the early sunlight. It looked beautiful. The shadows stretched smoothly over the smooth, shaven grass and the shrubs were plump and round like well-fed birds. Pride surged up inside him. He turned to look at Mike, Freckles, and Maggots, and saw that their faces, too, were alight with pleasure.

"They're my men," he reminded himself, "and I'm their leader."

"Good work, men," he said generously. "Good work. You can come round to my house for some lemonade, and then we'll get on to the next item on the agenda."

He strode off, and Maggots, Mike, and Freckles followed him, well content to be the followers of Jumbo Spencer.

5

♥♥♥

ROAD UNDER
REPAIR

The Jumbo Spencer Reform Club spent an hour in the orchard drinking lemonade and discussing future plans. But after a little while clamorous voices started in Jumbo's brain, and he began to feel restive and guilty. He saw Miss Mogg's soft, lined face as she had quavered out her wish for a zebra crossing. He remembered how sweetly she had smiled at him when he had told her he would see about it for her, and he could bear it no longer. He sprang to his feet.

"Come on," he said, "there's work to do."

Once they were up again, walking along the hot white lane to the village, he could feel his enthusiasm returning. He juggled carelessly with the paint brushes he was carrying. Maggots staggered in the rear with two large pots of paint and Freckles and Mike were carrying between them two long poles and two large boards. They marched briskly in step down the High Street until they came to a stop outside Miss Mogg's whitewashed cottage.

"Right. The boards, Mike!" said Jumbo. "One each side of us."

The boards were large and white, and painted on them in livid orange were the words "DANGER ROAD UNDER REPAIR." Between them Mike and Freckles set them up.

"We'll do this half of the road now," said Jumbo, "while the traffic uses the other side. Have you got the chalk and tape measure, Freckles?"

"They're here, Jumbo."

Freckles and Maggots both got down on their knees in the road and began measuring the stripes, while Jumbo sat down on the soft grass verge and watched them for a while. Then he fetched out his penknife and pried open the tins of paint. He began the agreeable task of stirring the thick, treacly liquid.

"We're ready, Jumbo," said Mike.

"Good. I'll do the white stripes and you do the black. Maggots and Freckles, you'd better keep your eyes open for traffic."

He knelt down in the road and began painting. It wasn't altogether satisfactory. The road was rather rough, and pieces of grit kept getting in the paint. Soon he was absorbed, his thoughts moving in a slow, steady rhythm with the strokes of the brush.

He was roused by a sudden violent screech of brakes

and looked up to see a lorry towering over him. The driver's face appeared at the window.

" 'Ere!" he said. "Wot's going on?"

"Road under repair," said Jumbo, straightening up. "Didn't you see the sign?"

"When it was too late I did," said the driver. "Coming down that hill on the bend you can't see it till it's too late. Dangerous, that's wot it is."

"I know," said Jumbo, "that's why we're making a zebra. It's an absolute death trap."

"Been some accidents, 'ave there?" asked the driver with interest.

"Not yet," said Jumbo darkly, "but it's only a matter of time."

"Anyway," said the driver, "oo told you to go making a zebra? It ain't your job."

"It is my job," Jumbo corrected him, "as President of the Jumbo Spencer Reform Club. There's a poor old lady living in that house," he pointed to the cottage, "who daren't even cross the road to go to the post office. In fact," he groped for a good phrase, "in fact the whole village lives in the shadow of fear."

A grin spread slowly over the driver's face.

"Yer meantersay you're making a zebra right off yer own bat?" he said admiringly. "Well, good luck ter yer, mate. That's wot I call inishative. But 'ave yer thought wot the perlice are going to say about it?"

"The police ought to be downright ashamed of themselves," said Jumbo severely. "They ought to do jobs like this themselves, and not leave it to us."

"You're right, they should!" said the driver warmly. "It's no jobs for kids. Well, good luck ter yer, mate! Cheerio! Yer want to move that sign 'igher up the road, though," he called warningly. And with an enormous roar the lorry started off again.

Jumbo was about to resume his painting when he noticed that Bert Stiggins and his gang were approaching.

"At the ready, men," Jumbo warned. "Here comes trouble."

Bert Stiggins was in an ugly mood. He and his gang were just returning from an interview with Mr. Bennet, which had been humiliating, to say the least. At the moment, Bert was of the opinion that any fate would be too good for Jumbo Spencer. He was also beginning to feel the effects of being up from four o'clock cutting trees.

He stopped about ten yards from the operation and stood taking in the scene. Five stripes had already been painted and Mike was just finishing off the sixth, which brought them approximately to the middle of the road.

Bert didn't say anything. He was in no mood for parleying. Jumbo Spencer had a way of talking that tied Bert up in knots. He merely stood there until the situation was quite clear to him. Then he turned in silence and went back up the High Street followed by his gang.

"Oh, Jumbo," said Maggots, "what do you think he's going to do?"

"Nothing, probably," said Jumbo briefly. "He hasn't got the brains. We'd better clear up now and go for dinner. Freckles, go and ask Miss Mogg if we can leave our things in her garden till after dinner."

He lay back on the verge and closed his eyes, inhaling the smell of new paint and wondering what was for dinner. If he had known what Bert Stiggins was doing at that very moment, he would perhaps have felt less relaxed.

Bert Stiggins and three of his gang were firmly wedged in the telephone booth at the top of the High Street. There was not much room to move and they were having difficulty turning the pages of the directory. Things were not made easier by the fact that none of them was very good at spelling.

"I tell you we want the P's," said Bert.

"But, Bert, Mr. Brown's name don't begin with P," objected Dick Perkins.

"I ain't ringing up Mr. Brown," said Bert.

"But Bert, you said you was ringing up the police, and Mr. Brown's the police," said Cyril Boot, whose head was crushed hard against the coin box and who was getting tired.

"Police!" exclaimed Bert scornfully. "He comes here about twice a week on a bicycle and you call him the police! Immediate action, that's wot we want. He wouldn't get here till next Thursday!"

"Oo are you going to ring up, then, Bert?" asked Dick, who also felt claustrophobia creeping over him.

"Pottingham Police Station," said Bert. Pottingham was a large town several miles away.

"Cor, Bert, had you better?" gasped Alf Martin, a small boy who was perhaps the most uncomfortable of

all because his head was wedged in between everybody else's shoulders and backs.

"Didn't you see wot he was doing?" demanded Bert hotly. "Painting a zebra, right across the High Street. It's against the law. You can't just go round painting zebras."

"P'raps they'll put him in prison, Bert," said Alf nervously.

"Shouldn't be surprised," said Bert. "Now, here we are. Here's the P's . . ."

For some minutes he turned pages and ran a grimy thumb down the columns, while the rest of the gang pushed restlessly against each other, struggling for more comfortable positions.

"Stop shoving, can't you?" said the exasperated Bert. "You've made me lose my place now. Alf and Cyril, you go outside. You can stop, Dick."

The other two pushed their way out and then stood with their faces squashed hard against the glass, anxious to miss nothing.

"Pottingham 666," said Bert. "Write it down, Dick, I might forget it. Now, where's the fourpence?"

He put the fourpence in the slot and slowly dialled the number.

There was a loud dialling tone and then a click.

"We're through!" cried Bert excitedly, jabbing Dick hard in the ribs. "Hello, hello!"

"Pottingham police, can I help you?" came a voice.

"Yes you can!" said Bert. "I'm ringing up to report a crime."

"Pottingham police, can I help you?" came the voice again, this time a little less patiently.

"Can't you hear me?" yelled Bert rudely. "I'm in Shoredale. This is Bert Stiggins speaking."

"Are you in a call box?" asked the voice at the other end of the line.

"Of course I am!" yelled Bert. "Fourpence this cost me!"

"Press Button A," came the voice wearily.

"Do what?" cried Bert. "She's barmy."

"Press Button A," said Dick. "Look!"

He pressed the button and the money clanged into the box.

"Now, can I help you?" said the voice crisply.

"I'm ringing up to report a crime," said Bert again.

"Very well, sir. I'll just take the particulars. If you'd like to give me the details . . . ?"

"It's Jumbo Spencer!" yelled Bert triumphantly, drunk with success.

"Who?" said the voice.

"Jumbo Spencer! He's painting a zebra from Miss Mogg's cottage to the post office. You'd better come quick, he's done half of it already."

There was a disappointing silence.

"Who's speaking?" asked the voice at last.

"It's me!" yelled Bert. "Bert Stiggins!"

"May I ask you how old you are?" asked the voice.

"Eleven," said Bert, "the same as Jumbo. Look, if you don't come quickly he'll get away!"

It took another five minutes for Bert to explain to the voice just exactly what was going on in Shoredale while the law slept, and by the end of it Bert was practically exhausted. He slammed the receiver down with relief.

"Police!" he said disgustedly to Dick. "They don't understand plain English!"

He stamped out of the booth.

"What happened? What did they say" clamored the gang, who had watched Bert gesticulating and shouting inside the booth in a state of fascinated hypnosis.

"They're sending someone down to investigate," said Bert nonchalantly.

"What, now?" gasped Cyril, peering down the road expectantly as if he hoped to see a squad of police cars come racing towards them.

"Soon as they can," said Bert. "We'll all dash home for dinner, then meet again here straight away. I don't want to miss this!"

They tore off in different directions. Within twenty minutes the whole gang was back at the top of the High Street with their last mouthful of pudding hardly swallowed.

Jumbo worked his way through his dinner in a more leisurely fashion. Afterwards he spent some time carving a slot in an empty cocoa tin and pasting on a label reading "The Jumbo Spencer Reform Club Fund." He had had the impression that Miss Mogg might wish to make a contribution.

He then spent some minutes before the glass trying

on a selection of bow ties presented to him by Maggots that morning. He selected one of brilliant scarlet which seemed to express his mood, and sauntered back to the village.

He noticed the Bert Stiggins gang grouped at the top of the High Street, but ignored them. Jumbo reached the zebra, and was about to give the word for work to commence, when his attention was attracted by a black car, approaching swiftly from the top of the High Street. He saw Bert Stiggins step into the road and wave wildly, and the car stopped. Jumbo saw that it was a police car. So did Mike and Freckles, and as the car began to move towards them, they automatically ranged themselves behind Jumbo.

The car stopped level with the half-painted crossing and two peak-capped policemen got out. Jumbo, watching them closely, saw that they were young and it seemed to him that one of them was trying not to smile.

"Now, then, which of you is Jumbo Spencer?" asked the taller of the two.

"I am," said Jumbo, taking a step forward.

"And what's all this?" asked the policeman, indicating the stripes on the road.

"A zebra," said Jumbo. "We haven't finished it yet."

The policeman took out a notebook.

"What's your address?" he asked.

Jumbo told him.

"We'd better go along there, then," he said. "Hop in, all of you."

He held open the back door of the car and they climbed in in silence and sat stiffly on the long shiny seat, conscious that by now half the village was watching them from doorways and windows. In the distance they could hear Bert and his gang yelling:

"Jumbo Spencer's being taken to prison! Jumbo's going to prison!"

The driver got in and the other policeman was just about to when a small figure came tearing down the High Street, legs flashing like pistons.

It was Maggots. She flung her arms in a Rugby tackle round the policeman's legs to stop herself, and they both went flying to the ground. Jumbo closed his eyes. When he opened them again the policeman had picked himself up and was pulling Maggots to her feet. Her face was dusty and streaked with tears.

"Don't take Jumbo away!" she sobbed. "D-don't put him in prison! He only did it because Miss Mogg was sc-scared to cross the road. Pleeeease!"

Her voice ended in a high-pitched wail and she broke out into sobs again.

"Now then, young lady, no one's going to prison," said the officer. "Come on, you come with us. Never been for a ride in a police car before, have you?"

He picked her up and got into the car, still holding her. Her sobs redoubled in strength. Jumbo sat staring in fascination at the policeman's back. The car started up and turned round back up the High Street.

"Put me off here," said the policeman who was hold-

ing Maggots. "I'll just have a word with this Bert Stiggins and make a few inquiries round the village."

He put Maggots down and got out. He walked to-
ward Bert and his gang, who came eagerly forward to
meet him.

Jumbo continued to stare after him. Across the back
of his dark blue tunic and trousers, unmistakable in the
bright sunlight, were two wide, white stripes.

6

JUMBO VERSUS THE POLICE

The Police car swished into the farmyard and the turkeys and hens flew off in a shower of feathers and alarm. It came to a standstill just in front of the farmhouse door.

"Jump out!" said the policeman. He got out himself and helped Maggots, while the other three climbed out of the back seat.

Jumbo's mother came to the door and stood there like a statue with her mouth wide open.

"Good afternoon, madam," said the officer. "I'm P. C. Jury. I just wanted to ask one or two questions."

"What has he done?" asked Jumbo's mother faintly.

"Oh, nothing we need worry about too much, Mrs. Spencer," said P. C. Jury. "Been taking the law into his own hands, that's all."

"W-won't you come in?" she said, leading the way

into the cool, whitewashed kitchen. They all sat down in a stiff little circle. Jumbo was still dazed, but now his brain was beginning to function again, and he sat sizing up P. C. Jury and preparing his speech. The constable was explaining to Jumbo's mother what they had been doing.

"And now, what's your side of the story, young man?" he asked, turning to Jumbo.

Jumbo got off his chair. He could speak better standing.

"I think I had better begin at the beginning," he said slowly.

"Yes, do that," said the officer pleasantly.

So Jumbo launched into an account of the Jumbo Spencer Reform Club, and how it had been formed and what its aims were. When he came to the part where Miss Mogg had asked for a zebra crossing, he nearly brought tears to his own eyes with his description of her sad life, never being able to go across to the post office for stamps or sweets, and, glancing quickly at Maggots, he saw that her eyes were actually swimming. Unfortunately, P. C. Jury did not look at all close to tears, so Jumbo plunged with renewed zest into his story.

He had just finished when the other policeman came in. He introduced himself as P. C. Grey, and Jumbo had a breathing space while P. C. Jury repeated to him what Jumbo had just told him.

"Hmmmm," said P. C. Grey. "I've been making a few inquiries in the village. It looks as if there really should be a zebra crossing there. Quite a lot of people came forward and said so. I saw this Miss Mogg, too, and she verified that it was she who had told the boy she would like a crossing. I must say the poor old soul seemed genuinely terrified of crossing the road."

Jumbo's confidence mounted as he heard all this.

"There should have been one years ago," he said.

P. C. Jury turned.

"Now then," he said sternly, "the less said by you the better. It doesn't matter what the rights and wrongs of the case are, it's not your business to go round taking the law into your own hands. If you thought there should be a zebra, your job was to report the matter to us, not go painting one yourself. What if everyone did it? The roads would look like a snakes and ladders board."

"I suppose they would," said Jumbo thoughtfully.

"I hope this will be a lesson to you," said P. C. Jury. "Next time you feel like putting up a bollard or making a traffic island, just have a word with us first, will you?"

"Oh certainly," agreed Jumbo. "Yes, I will, thank you. I don't think we were making a very good job of it, anyway. The road was too gritty."

"Just as a matter of interest," said P. C. Grey, "what were you going to do about the flashing beacons?"

"I'm afraid that was rather a snag," explained Jumbo. "We couldn't have flashing lights, and it didn't seem to matter too much, anyway, because Miss Mogg never goes out after dark. We were going to paint two posts black and white and have two orange balloons on top."

"Two orange balloons?"

There was a pause, and then he burst out laughing. In a moment P. C. Jury joined him. The two policemen stood there roaring until they both had to bring out

handkerchiefs to wipe their eyes. Jumbo was not particularly flattered by this, but at the same time glad to see them in so good a humor. He felt that to go to prison would be bad publicity for a social reformer and leader of men.

"A very ingenious son you've got there, Mrs. Spencer," said P. C. Jury at last. "Wants some watching, I should think. Now then, what about cleaning up the mess you've made on the road?"

He looked at them all severely.

"Isn't Jumbo going to prison, then?" whispered Maggots incredulously. She had not really followed anything that had gone on.

"Not this time," said P. C. Jury. "But someone's going to have to clean up that mess."

"As a matter of fact . . ." began P. C. Grey slowly. The other policeman looked at him.

"As a matter of fact, I've already arranged that. Our little informer—what's his name—Bert Stiggins and some of his friends. I told him that there would be some men coming later in the week to make a proper zebra crossing, and I'd take it as a favor if he'd get the road cleaned up straight away. I told him we'd call back later on today to make sure it was done."

P. C. Jury tried to suppress a smile.

"We'll be on our way, then," he said. "Sorry to have troubled you, Mrs. Spencer."

But Jumbo was still staring dumbfounded at P. C. Grey.

"Sir," he said hoarsely, "sir. Did you say a proper zebra crossing? Did you say there's going to be a proper one?"

P. C. Grey paused in the doorway.

"I think it's more than likely," he said. "Good-bye."

He disappeared, and the two white stripes across his back were plainly visible in the sunlight before he stepped into the car and with a roar it shot out into the lane.

Jumbo felt a tingling sensation running up his spine and right out at the roots of his hair.

"A real zebra!" he whispered. "Did you hear that?"

He felt a lump in his throat like the one he always had when he heard "Land of Hope and Glory." He had won a reform for the village of Shoredale. He, Jumbo Spencer, had forced the police to give Shoredale a zebra crossing. He hardly knew himself how he had done it, but it was true. He really was a social reformer!

"Oh, Mum!" he groaned, overcome with emotion. "Let's have some lemonade! I'm half dead after all that!"

For the rest of that day the whole village was in a state of wild rumor and excitement. Bert Stiggins and his gang were busy till tea-time cleaning the road, surrounded by a curious crowd, to whom they willingly gave their version of the story, which was that Jumbo Spencer was going to prison later on, but was at present out on bail. They couldn't be sure how long he would be in, but they thought it might be a year, with six months each for Mike, Freckles, and Maggots.

Miss Mogg sat in her window between the lace curtains and to one side of her aspidistra plant and waved shyly to the crowds who had gathered at the scene of excitement. She even had her tea in the window, in case she should miss anything.

At about five o'clock the police car swished to a standstill outside her cottage, and P. C. Jury and P. C. Grey got out and inspected the state of the road. Bert and his gang had not been very successful, and the road was a messy-looking gray, but the two policemen appeared pleased and soon got back in their car and shot off again with the satisfying roar you expect of a police car.

Just before six o'clock the gang went down to the village. Jumbo was carrying a collection tin and a rolled up poster.

"Remember," he said between his teeth as they appeared at the top of the High Street and everyone turned to look, "we walk straight through. Not a word. If anyone asks anything, just say 'No comment.' "

"N-n-no comment?" said Mike, puzzled.

"Yes, it means you have nothing to say," explained Jumbo. "Now, come on. Just act natural."

They went forward and a silence fell over the village as they passed. Bert Stiggins and his gang stood and watched them, searching their faces in vain for any sign of emotion. Beyond the Pump was a huge, spreading oak tree, whose broad trunk served as a village notice-board. Here the little procession stopped.

"Nails, Freckles," whispered Jumbo out of the corner of his mouth, producing a hammer from his pocket.

He unrolled the poster he had under his arm, and with slow deliberate strokes proceeded to drive a nail into each corner. The whole village watched in silence. There was no sound but those loud, slow strokes.

When it was done, Jumbo whispered, "Right! Disperse! But remember—no comment!"

He went off alone up the street while the others made their separate ways home. Some village boys followed Mike, but all their questions and taunts received no response. He plodded stolidly on to his own house, where at last he faced the little knot of followers, thought hard for a minute while he remembered the phrase, and then finally said: "N-n-n-no c-comment!" and went in and shut the door.

Everyone else was crowding round the oak tree to read the notice. It was headed THE JUMBO SPENCER REFORM CLUB President—JUMBO SPENCER. Underneath it said:

"This Club has been formed with the intention of reforming the village of Shoredale and righting all wrongs. Already one blow has been struck for freedom. Shoredale is to have a zebra crossing. Jumbo Spencer has come to an understanding with the police about this matter. He now intends to make further reforms. All those who agree should attend a meeting by the Pump at 6 pm tomorrow evening. (Signed) ——," and here was an illegible scrawl which was obviously Jumbo's new signature.

The crowd gasped.

"Gone to prison, has he?" said Mr. Jefferson with heavy sarcasm.

Bert slunk away.

Meanwhile Jumbo himself had retired early with a light supper of bread and honey, sausage rolls, walnut cakes, and milk, and was sitting up in bed with a book on social reform propped on his knees. In the distance a lawn-mower began to whirr and a blackbird was singing. He closed his eyes for a moment and the two sounds began to weave together into music that was like every other summer evening he had ever known. He opened his eyes, closed them again, and the book on social reform slid slowly down. Jumbo Spencer was asleep.

7

THE VISIT

The next morning Jumbo could not decide what to wear for his interview with Mr. Bennet. He was torn between the gray suit, blue checked shirt, boater, and white gloves, and his oldest jeans, with an orange and green striped tee shirt that his mother would not allow him to wear in public because it was too "loud."

He knew that Mr. Bennet was a very famous man, a writer and philosopher. He also knew that he had a very low opinion of the younger generation. He was always saying that in his day young people had to fight for things—they didn't just have them handed to them on a plate.

If Jumbo went in his best clothes, although he felt that this would put him on an equal footing with Mr. Bennet, it might also give the impression that Jumbo lived a life of idle luxury, and was what Mr. Bennet would call "spoonfed." On the other hand, if he went in his old clothes, at least he would look like a rebel, but Mr. Bennet might think he was disrespectful.

The decision was a difficult one. In the end Jumbo put on the lime green and orange shirt and blue jeans. The colors made him feel dashing.

He went down to breakfast.

"Is that you, Jumbo?" called his mother.

He often wondered who else she thought it was. She asked him every morning, just to be on the safe side, he supposed.

"Yes, it's me," said Jumbo wearily. Perhaps one day someone else would come down in his place and give his mother a real surprise. She came in.

"Heavens, Jumbo! What have you got on?" she said.

"My orange and green shirt and jeans, Mum," said Jumbo patiently.

"You've got plenty of other things clean," said his mother. "I never saw such a horrible color scheme."

"I like it," said Jumbo. "It's different."

"I should hope so," said his mother. "It makes me feel quite ill. And that reminds me. Mr. Bennet was on television last night."

"Oh?" said Jumbo, his interest aroused. "What was he talking about?"

"The usual," said his mother. "He was going on about the younger generation, and their bad manners, and the terrible way they dress. And I must say, looking at you,

Jumbo, I can see what he meant. Jumbo, where are you going?"

Jumbo pushed back his plate and rose wearily.

"Up to change, Mum."

"I don't know," he heard her say as he went, "I really don't know!"

He was hardly halfway up when she called him back.

"Here's a letter for you, Jumbo. Postmarked Pottingham."

Jumbo came slowly down and took the letter. She watched him open it. It was headed "Pottingham Constabulary" in bold, black Olde English writing.

It was to thank him for drawing their attention to the need for a zebra crossing in Shoredale, and to assure him that one would be forthcoming with the least possible delay.

It went on to say that while the Chief Constable admired Jumbo's public-spiritedness in attempting to make one himself, they hoped that in the future he would place more confidence in the police, and make his suggestions to them first. It was signed "W. S. Bagshott, Chief Constable."

Jumbo read it four times, admired the way he had been addressed as Jumbo Spencer Esq., and then handed it to his mother.

"Oh, Jumbo!" she cried. "How lovely! What a nice letter! What a nice man Mr. Bagshott must be. Well, I am pleased."

Jumbo was not much impressed by his mother's enthusiasm. He had made a study of adults' behavior, and
had noticed that they had practically no sense of justice
at all. While Jumbo was in trouble over painting the
zebra she had called it "a lot of silly nonsense." Now,
the moment a letter came with an important-looking
crest on it and signed by a Chief Constable, everything
was all right. He sighed. Mothers certainly took some
understanding.

"It would be nice to put this on the notice-board in
the village for everyone to see, wouldn't it, Jumbo?"
she fussed, reading it again. She wanted the villagers to
know that her Jumbo had more sense than some of them
made out. Jumbo realized this, and because he was sorry
she had been upset by the episode with the police the
day before, he agreed.

"All right, Mum," he said, smiling at her. "I'll do it
on my way."

Jumbo felt his mood change as he changed his clothes.
He felt more important and a little wiser in the gray
suit and boater, but he was not sure that he felt quite so
courageous. He changed the white handkerchief in his
top pocket for a violent red silk square of his mother's
that matched his bow tie, and immediately felt better.
He left quietly by the back way in case his mother saw
him and made any remarks that might undermine his
self-confidence.

As he went he kept repeating over and over to himself, "I am a great reformer and a leader of men," and hoped that he would remember this when he came face to face with Mr. Bennet. At heart Jumbo was looking forward to the interview. He respected Mr. Bennet, and felt that he was a worthy adversary. He had outgrown such opponents as Bert Stiggins. This was a real challenge.

The sensation he caused by strolling down the High Street left nothing to be desired. Everyone nudged and whispered and stared, but he noticed there was less sniggering than there had been when he first appeared in his bow tie. This meant that they were beginning to realize that he was someone to be reckoned with.

He nailed the letter strongly and noisily on to the oak tree trunk and then strolled on. He looked with appreciation at the church and leaning tombstones as he passed them, and thought that when he grew up he, too, would have an ivy-covered house in a graveyard. It was so quiet, and had the right atmosphere for thinking. There was no wonder that Mr. Potter managed to think of a different sermon for every Sunday.

The rooks were gossiping roughly in the high elms. They were rude birds and their nests were shaggy and untidy, but they were Jumbo's favorites. He had often toyed with the idea of taming a rook and keeping it in his bedroom. He liked the idea of strolling through the village in the evenings with the rook perched on his wrist.

He heard his name called, and saw Mr. Potter.

"Good morning, Spencer," he said. "You do look— smart."

He paused slightly before the last word, as though at a loss for a word suitable to describe Jumbo's striking appearance.

"Good morning, Mr. Potter," said Jumbo. "I was just admiring your graves."

"Oh, er, thank you," said Mr. Potter, who was not used to people admiring this particular aspect of his church. "Going somewhere special?"

"Only to Mr. Bennet's," said Jumbo casually. "I just wanted a word with him."

"Oh," said the vicar again. Somehow conversation with Jumbo Spencer always left him at a loss for words, which was strange, because usually he was a very talk-ative man.

"I must congratulate you on the success of your re-form club, Jumbo," he said. "I hear we're to have a ze-bra crossing. Very good work. Very good work!"

"Well, it's a start," agreed Jumbo. "How are your reforms going?" he asked chattily.

"Oh, not so bad," said Mr. Potter. "I can't claim any such startling results as yours, though."

"Never mind," said Jumbo sympathetically. "Some things do take longer than others. If you'll excuse me, sir, I think I'd better be getting along. I want to be sure to catch him."

"Yes, yes of course," said Mr. Potter. "Good-bye—and good luck!"

"Good-bye," said Jumbo. "Good luck with your reforms, too!"

Mr. Potter stared after his retreating figure, and shook his head wonderingly.

"I don't know," he said to himself, "I really don't know!"

It took only two or three minutes to reach the high, wrought-iron gates of the drive to Shoredale Manor. Jumbo crossed the road and stood for a moment, hands clasped behind him, surveying them. He had been in the grounds on many occasions, but it had always been by way of scaling a tree and dropping over the wall, or crawling through a hole in the hedge. He passed between the gates, enjoying the sensation of being a legitimate visitor. It occurred to him that Mr. Bennet might not even recognize him in these clothes, which in some ways would be a good thing.

It was nearly ten minutes before he emerged on to the wide lawns in front of the manor itself. He felt suddenly small and inconspicuous on that wide, empty space, and hoped that Mr. Bennet was not looking out of the windows. He lifted the grinning brass door knocker and rapped loudly.

"I am a social reformer and a leader of men," he reminded himself.

He drew himself up, and the door opened. It was Mr.

Bennet's manservant, Briggs. He looked very surprised to see Jumbo.

"Good morning," said Jumbo politely. "Is Mr. Bennet available, please?"

"Young Spencer, isn't it?" said Briggs rudely, with-

out replying to his question. "Hardly recognized you."

"I wish to speak to Mr. Bennet on an important matter," said Jumbo, determined to keep his dignity and not be led into idle conversation with Briggs.

"Oh, do you!" said Briggs sourly. His views on the younger generation were much the same as those of his master, although they were based on rather different reasons. "Well, I can't say that I think he'll want to speak to *you*."

"Perhaps you would let him know I'm here," suggested Jumbo. "You might tell him it's to do with a suggestion of Mr. Potter's," he added, with a flash of inspiration. After all, he reflected, it had been the vicar's idea that he should get a youth club and playing-fields for Shoredale.

"I'll tell him," said Briggs after a long look at Jumbo. "But I don't say as it'll do any good."

The door closed and Jumbo was face to face with the knocker again. He waited patiently, filling in the time by wondering who had clipped the bushes in front of the manor into the shape of peacocks. He felt sure that it could not have been Briggs, who did not seem to Jumbo to have enough soul for that kind of work. The door opened.

"He'll see you," said Briggs. "You're to come in."

Jumbo stepped inside, his heart thudding. Briggs led the way through a dim, panelled hall, and opened a door on his right.

"You're to wait in here," he said. He gave Jumbo a

little shove inside and closed the door. Jumbo took a few steps forward. The door opened again.

"And don't touch anything!" said Briggs rudely. "Hands off!"

The door closed. Jumbo began to breathe again and looked round with interest. He was in the library. The walls were lined with shelves, and thousands of books, most of them bound in red leather, stood shoulder to shoulder, hushed and secretive. He had the strangest feeling that they knew he was there.

Above the fireplace was a portrait. He walked over and stood beneath it, hands clasped behind his back. He rather thought it was meant to be Mr. Bennet, but he couldn't be too sure because it was all made up of triangles and squares, and seemed to be trying to show both sides of his face at once.

"Like it?" he heard a voice behind him.

Jumbo wheeled round, and came face to face with Mr. Bennet.

8

ꙮꙮꙮ

JUMBO MAKES
A BARGAIN

"I was just trying to make up my mind," said Jumbo.

"Good," said Mr. Bennet. "Good. Take your time."

Jumbo went on staring at the picture for a few more minutes because he felt that this was expected of him. Mr. Bennet did not speak. It was very quiet. In the end Jumbo gave a sigh and turned away.

"Well?" said Mr. Bennet.

"I do like it," said Jumbo.

"Why?" asked Mr. Bennet. His eyes were gray and very piercing. They tended to make him look rather fierce.

"It's not boring like most pictures," said Jumbo. "Every time you look at it you see something different."

"Good," said Mr. Bennet. "Now sit down and tell me what you want."

Jumbo sat in the nearest chair. It was an unfortunate

chair because it was a high-winged armchair and practically buried him. It was difficult to feel dignified in that kind of chair. Mr. Bennet remained standing. He was wearing a plum-colored velvet jacket of which Jumbo approved very strongly. No one else in Shoredale wore plum-colored jackets. He also wore a bow tie, and was at that moment looking rather keenly at Jumbo's own.

"My name is Jumbo Spencer," began Jumbo.

"Ah!" said Mr. Bennet. "Of course. We've met before, I think. And wait a minute, isn't it Jumbo Spencer who's been painting zebras in the High Street?"

"That's me, sir," said Jumbo modestly.

"What's it all about?" inquired Mr. Bennet.

"I'm trying to reform Shoredale," explained Jumbo. "I just dealt with the small things first. I want to get to grips with the big problems now."

"You do, do you?" said Mr. Bennet. "And how do I enter into it?"

"I have come to appeal to you," said Jumbo. He slid out of the chair and stood upright. "The village needs a hall, sir, for bazaars and meetings and things, and so that we can have a youth club. And we need playing-fields and a pavilion."

Mr. Bennet continued to look at him, his face expressionless.

"And so," said Jumbo, "I have decided to ask you for some help. I could never raise thousands and thousands of pounds on my own, and that's what it will cost."

"I see," said Mr. Bennet. "You want me to put my

hand in my pockets and dig out thousands and thousands of pounds for you. Is that it?"

"Yes, please," said Jumbo. "We would be very grateful, sir."

"Good, that's very gratifying," said Mr. Bennet.
"What makes you think I should pay for all this?"

"Several reasons, sir," said Jumbo.

"I'll hear them, please," said Mr. Bennet. He sat down
in a winged, brocade chair and stretched out his legs.
He put the palms of his hands together and waited.

"For one thing," said Jumbo, "you're very rich."

"Am I?" asked Mr. Bennet.

"Yes, sir. Everyone in the village says you've got
more money than you know what to do with."

"Do they!" said Mr. Bennet. "It wouldn't be more
than *they* knew what to do with, I feel sure."

"For another thing," said Jumbo, who had not sat up
half the night making notes by the light of a torch
propped on the blankets for nothing, "money doesn't
mean much to a man like you."

"Oh? Why not?"

"Because you're a thinker," said Jumbo. "You have
your mind on higher things. Money doesn't mean much
to me, either, sir."

"Oh?" said Mr. Bennet. "Am I to take it that you are
a thinker, too, then?"

"Yes, sir," said Jumbo. "I'm always thinking. I spend
hours thinking."

"Remarkable," said Mr. Bennet. "Go on."

"We'll forget about the money for a moment," said Jumbo. "Then there's the fame."

"Fame?" said Mr. Bennet.

"Yes, sir. We'd call it 'The William Bennet Memorial Hall,' sir, and 'The William Bennet Memorial Playing-Fields,' and 'The William Bennet Memorial Pavilion.' There would be three brass plaques, all with your name on."

"Very comforting," said Mr. Bennet, "but I'm not dead yet."

"No, sir, but you will be, sooner or later. You're quite old."

Mr. Bennet said nothing. Like the vicar, he was at a loss.

"Not all that old," said Jumbo, not wishing to be unkind. "But quite old. You've got to look ahead."

"Are there any more reasons?" inquired Mr. Bennet mildly.

"One more," said Jumbo.

"And what is that?"

Jumbo looked him straigtht in the eye.

"I think you'd enjoy it, sir," he said simply.

There was a silence. They regarded each other steadily.

"Would I?" asked Mr. Bennet at last.

"Yes, you would," said Jumbo. His enthusiasm began to work up. "Just think of it! A huge hall, with a shiny floor like this one, and a stage with blue velvet curtains and footlights! And a beautiful white pavilion on the playing-fields, with a veranda and lots of deck chairs where everyone could sit and watch the cricket. And I could put on plays in the winter and everyone could come and see them. And I could hold bazaars and meetings and no one would ever be bored again!"

"I can see that *you* would enjoy it," remarked Mr. Bennet.

"And *you* would!" persisted Jumbo. "You'd feel really good, like I did when I got the zebra crossing. It's the best feeling I've ever had!"

Mr. Bennet looked at Jumbo. His eyes were alight and his bow tie was lopsided. He was remembering a boy years ago, who had stood before his mother and father as Jumbo was standing before him now, crying, "But, Father, I don't want to go to the party! I'm writing a book, and it's going to change the whole world! I've got to write it!" And that boy had really believed it, just as Jumbo believed in his reforms. Mr. Bennet sighed.

Suddenly he looked up and saw Jumbo watching him with interest. He pulled himself together.

"You know my views on the younger generation, I think," he said sternly.

"Yes, sir," said Jumbo. "You think they're rude, selfish and lazy, and expect to be spoon-fed."

"And it's true," said Mr. Bennet. "Absolutely true. This is just typical. You decided that you'd like a village hall and all kinds of things to make life pleasant, and what do you do? Instead of buckling to and doing something about it yourself, you come to me and ask me for the money, as if it were as easy as that. It won't do. It won't do."

"But, sir," cried Jumbo, "I worked it out. Even if I gave a play at the Memorial Theatre every night for the whole holidays and everyone in the village came every night, there still wouldn't be enough in a hundred years!"

"You worked it out, did you?" said Mr. Bennet.

"Yes, sir, I worked out all kinds of things. I didn't want to have to ask you, but it would need thousands and thousands of pounds!"

Jumbo looked desperate. Strangely enough, Mr. Bennet really believed him. He believed this boy really had tried to work out how he could make thousands and thousands of pounds on his own. He felt a little dazed.

"It's impossible unless you help!" cried Jumbo.

"Help!" said Mr. Bennet, clutching at a straw. "Ah, now, that's a very different thing. I understood that you wanted me to pay for the whole thing. Now help, that's a very different matter."

"Is it?" cried Jumbo joyfully. "Oh, is it?"

"I'll tell you what," said Mr. Bennet thoughtfully, "I'll make you an offer. I don't mind helping lively, enthusiastic people with minds of their own, but I won't help lazy layabouts who expect everything to be handed to them on a plate. Is that clear?"

"Oh yes, sir," cried Jumbo.

"Then I'll tell you what. Tomorrow I am going

abroad for a month. If during that time you can earn fifty pounds, entirely by your own effort, then I'll contribute the rest. Is that fair?"

"Oh, Mr. Bennet!" cried Jumbo. "It's very fair! It's marvellous!"

"By your own efforts, mind you," said Mr. Bennet sternly. "I shall trust you, Jumbo, not to accept money from older people unless you and your friends have really earned it. Is that a promise?"

"Oh yes!" cried Jumbo again.

His ears were singing and his heart was thudding. The old poetry was beginning to run through his head like music, and he wanted to tear out of the house and down to the village, shouting at the top of his voice.

"Very well," said Mr. Bennet, taking out his watch. "Now you will have to go. I'm expecting a visitor. I will see you here, in this room, exactly one month from to-day. If you can show me fifty pounds that you can honestly say you have earned, the village hall is yours."

"And the playing-fields? And the pavilion?"

"And the playing-fields. And the pavilion."

Jumbo let out a deep breath.

"Thank you, sir," he said.

Mr. Bennet followed him out of the library and to the front door. Here Jumbo turned and held out his hand. Solemnly they shook hands.

"You'll never regret it, sir," said Jumbo. Then he turned and walked over the wide lawn, his legs trembling.

Mr. Bennet looked after him, suddenly realizing what he had promised.

"I don't know," he said under his breath, "I really don't know!"

And that made three.

Jumbo's greatest difficulty for the rest of that day was to control the torrent of schemes and ideas that swept through his mind. The Jumbo Spencer Reform Club collection box held 18s. 4d. That meant that in the next month £49 1s. 8d. must be earned. According to Jumbo's calculations, this in turn meant that he would have to average £12 5s. 5d. a week. A second season of the Jumbo Spencer Memorial Theatre was obviously not the answer to this problem.

At six o'clock when Jumbo sauntered down the High Street wearing a yellow shirt and black bow tie, nearly everyone in Shoredale was by the Pump waiting. By now the village was so convinced of Jumbo's powers, that had he informed them that he intended to have the Albert Hall moved brick by brick to Shoredale as a youth center, they would have believed him.

They listened intently while Jumbo told them about Mr. Bennet's promise.

"And now, I am asking for your co-operation," he said. "I promised Mr. Bennet not to accept money for nothing. So we want grown-ups to give us the chance to earn the money, and children to help us earn it."

There were cheers and loud assurances that everyone

in the village (with the exception of Bert Stiggins and his gang) was on his side.

"I have founded the Jumbo Spencer Employment Agency," Jumbo announced. A gasp ran through the crowd. "On this sheet of paper, anyone under the age of sixteen who wants to help can sign his name and say what kind of work he wants to do. On this other sheet, people who want jobs doing should put down what the job is, when they want it done, and how much they want to pay."

This fresh evidence of Jumbo's ingenuity brought another round of applause, amid which he stepped down from his soapbox and supervised the signing of the two sheets of the Jumbo Spencer Employment Agency. He then took them away with him to study. It seemed that nearly everyone in the village needed something doing. Gardens needed weeding, sheds needed clearing out, fences needed painting, groceries needed delivering, eggs needed collecting and babies needed sitting.

Jumbo had scored again.

9

KIDNAPPED!

Within two days everything was organized and things were running smoothly and according to plan. Already three cocoa tins were full of funds, and Jumbo was just beginning to feel that life was becoming boring again, when on Saturday evening there was some unexpected excitement.

Jumbo had spent a busy day organizing a variety of activities in the village. Over two pounds for the club fund had been raised and several children were baby-sitting that evening so he could count upon more to come.

After tea he went into the orchard with a book. He propped himself up against a favorite tree with a jug of lemonade close to hand, and settled down to a pleasant evening. It must have been an hour later, when the shadows were stretching and the air cooling, that he heard

the alarmed flurrying from the farmyard that meant the
arrival of unexpected visitors.

Moments later he saw Maggots running towards him,
her hair flying.

"Jumbo, oh, Jumbo, come quickly!" she gasped, and
burst into tears.

Jumbo sighed and put down his book.

"Shut up bawling, Maggots," he said good-humor-
edly. "It doesn't do any good, you know."

"Oh, Jumbo," sobbed Maggots, "come quickly!"

"Come where?" inquired Jumbo.

"To Mrs. Turnbull's. Quickly, before she gets home!"

"What for?" he asked.

"Someone's stolen the baby!" screamed Maggots desperately. "It's gone!"

Jumbo catapulted to his feet.

"What! Why on earth didn't you say so? Come on!"

He raced through the orchard and Maggotts followed him, sobbing and gasping for breath. They didn't stop until they reached Mrs. Turnbull's cottage on Shepherd's Lane.

Jumbo marched inside.

"Where was the baby?" he asked. "Are you sure it's not hiding somewhere?"

"In there!" Maggots pointed to a door, and Jumbo opened it and went through. It was a ground floor room looking out over the garden, and the windows were wide open. Under the windows was an empty pink cot. He looked round the room. The baby couldn't possibly be hiding. He doubted if it could have got through the window, but he looked over the sill to make sure. There was no sign of it, but he did notice that the flowers in the bed under the window were crushed and broken. Someone had been standing there.

Jumbo thought quickly. This, he realized, was a crisis. A lost baby could spell death to the Jumbo Spencer Employment Agency. He looked at his watch. It was nearly eight o'clock.

"What time did Mrs. Turnbull say she would be back?" he asked.

"Nine o'clock!" wailed Maggots. "We must find it, Jumbo, we must!"

"Of course," said Jumbo.

He set off down Shepherd's Lane. Near the end of it

was a tumbledown wooden hut surrounded by nettles. Jumbo walked quietly on the grass verge and softly approached the hut. He crept round to the back, and put his eye to a hole in the wood caused by a missing knot. Almost immediately a baby started crying.

Jumbo could see it lying in a folded sack in an empty seed box. He could also see Bert Stiggins, Dick Perkins, and Cyril Boot. Jumbo thought the scene worth watching for a little while.

"For goodness' sake shut it up, Cyril," said Bert irritably. "We shall have the whole village here."

"How?" asked Cyril helplessly, getting up and standing with his arms dangling.

"Didn't you bring the lemonade and buns?" demanded Bert. "Give it some of that. It'll be hungry, I expect. Those things need feeding every half-hour. Funny, ain't it?" he said, eyeing the baby speculatively. "You wouldn't think they'd got room inside them. Wish I had!"

Cyril took down from a shelf a bottle of lemonade and a paper bag. The baby's crying increased to a full-throated roaring.

"Oh, hurry up!" snapped Bert. "Put the bottle in its mouth."

Cyril obediently unstopped the bottle and bent over the baby. He made a clumsy movement in the direction of its mouth, missed, and sent a fizzing shower all over its face and clothes. It yelled. Bert Stiggins put his fingers in his ears and groaned.

"Pick it up!" he yelled.

He grabbed the lemonade bottle, put it to his own lips, and took a long swig, while Cyril made several unsuccessful attempts to pick the baby up. Every time his hot red face drew near, the baby redoubled its yells and flailed the air with its tiny fists.

In desperation, Cyril made a final lunge, and picked it up. For perhaps five seconds he stood there holding it,

and then as suddenly put it down in the seed box again.

"It's no good, Bert," he wailed, "I can't hold it! It wriggles. I might drop it and break it!"

"Scared of a baby!" sneered Bert. "I'll do it."

He took another swig from the lemonade bottle and approached the baby. It seemed to him that its mouth occupied more than half its face. He hesitated.

"I think I'll try it with a bun, first," he said, "and then give it a drink afterwards to wash it down with. Give us a bun, Dick."

Dick handed him a bun from the bag. Bert eyed it.

"It won't want all this," he decided. He took a large mouthful himself, and then held the bun invitingly near the baby's crimson face. It screamed louder than ever.

"Come on," said Bert invitingly. "Good baby, come on then. Good baby."

He gave it a little pat as if it were a dog. The baby ignored the bun and its mouth yawned to even larger proportions.

"Little brat!" said Bert in disgust. He took another bite at the bun. "What's wrong with it?"

"If it don't stop soon, someone'll hear it," said Dick Perkins gloomily. "We've got to keep it quiet at least another hour, until Mrs. Turnbull's home. And it'll have to be kept quiet while we put it back again."

"What do you want to do, then, sing nursery rhymes to it?" asked Bert sarcastically through a mouthful of bun.

"That's what my mum does when my kid sister bawls," offered Cyril Boot. "It usually works."

There was a silence. Bert Stiggins looked at his shoes, then at the bawling baby, then back at his shoes. He could bear it no longer.

"All right!" he yelled in desperation. "We'll all sing one together. Ready?"

"What are we singing?" inquired Dick.

Bert thought a minute.

" 'Baa, baa, black sheep,' " he ground through his teeth at last. "I'll count to three, and then we'll all start. All of us!" He glared fiercely at the other two.

"One, two, three!"

"Baa, baa, black sheep, have you any wool?" they chorused. Their faces were red and they tried not to look at each other. They dreaded to think what would happen if anyone ever found out about this. The door opened. No one noticed. The baby bawled lustily.

"And one for the little boy that cries down the lane . . . " they tailed off lamely.

There was a short silence. Jumbo clapped his hands.

"Very nice," he said approvingly.

They whipped round. Jumbo stood with his hands in his pockets, regarding them with an amused smile.

"Try 'Little Miss Muffet,' " he suggested. "Girls like that one."

Bert made a sound that was between a groan and a scream of pain, and the other two stood with mouths ajar, dumbfounded. Jumbo stooped and picked up the baby. Its clothes were grimy and its face filthy and streaked with tears. Miraculously, its screams changed to whimpers, and then died away altogether. Still no one spoke. Jumbo moved towards the door.

Bert made a desperate movement towards him and got up.

"Jumbo!" he croaked.

Jumbo turned and looked inquiringly at him.

"Jumbo, where are you going?"

"To take the baby back," said Jumbo. He again started for the door.

"Jumbo!" Bert almost yelled. Again he turned.

"Jumbo, you won't . . . you won't tell anyone?" he blurted, his face agonized.

"I shall have to tell Mrs. Turnbull," said Jumbo thoughtfully, "to explain how its clothes got so wet and dirty. And, of course, she's bound to tell the police. Kidnapping's a serious offense, you know."

"We didn't kidnap it!" cried Bert. "We—we borrowed it."

"Borrowed it?" said Jumbo. "What for?"

"To annoy you, Jumbo," said Bert at last in a small voice. "It was only a joke!"

"Oh, I don't mind taking it as a joke," said Jumbo easily. "It's Mrs. Turnbull who won't see the humor of it. Mothers are funny about babies, and this one is rather wet and dirty."

"You do see that it was a joke, don't you, Jumbo?" pleaded Bert.

"Oh, yes!" said Jumbo heartily. "Funniest thing I've seen for years. Wait till I tell them in the village about you trying to feed it with lemonade and buns, and then singing lullabies to it—'Baa, baa, black sheep!'" He laughed merrily.

Bert Stiggins had tears in his eyes.

"Don't tell, Jumbo!" he whispered. "Don't tell! I'll never hear the last of it!"

Jumbo looked at him thoughtfully for a moment, savoring his discomfiture.

"Of course," he said, "I could slip some clean things on the baby and get Maggots to wash these and take them back later. She could tell Mrs. Turnbull something got spilt on them. It's true, anyway."

"Oh, Jumbo, could you?" cried Bert.

"I *could*," said Jumbo speculatively.

"I'll do anything you like, Jumbo," said Bert. "Honest."

"I know you will," said Jumbo. "I should think so, too. 'Baa, baa, black sheep!' It's just a matter of thinking what I want you to do."

There was a silence but for the long, shuddering breaths of the baby.

"I know," announced Jumbo. "Mr. Green's garden!"

"Mr. Green's garden!" shouted Bert. "But it's like a jungle, Jumbo!"

"Of course," said Jumbo placidly. "He's been in hospital a year. Weeds grow quickly, you know. And lawns. And hedges. But he said he'd give five pounds to the fund if we dug it for him and made a really good job of it. You'd make a good job of it, wouldn't you, Bert?"

Cyril and Dick turned desperately to Bert. They would have dug Hampstead Heath to prevent news of this adventure leaking out.

"Yes, Jumbo," said Bert in a strangled voice.

"Good, that's settled then," said Jumbo heartily. "Report to me in the barn on Monday morning, nine sharp. Good-bye!"

The next minute he was gone. They stood motionless, listening to his whistling as it grew fainter and fainter down the lane. The tune he was whistling was "Baa, baa, black sheep."

10

A NEW VENTURE

One morning about a fortnight after his interview with Mr. Bennet, Jumbo Spencer woke up feeling full of energy and a vague restlessness. The moment he sat up in bed he felt that something important must happen soon, or he would die of boredom. He leaned out of the window and sniffed the cold air. Autumn was coming. Soon the leaves would be foxy red and brown, and bitter bonfire smoke would drift across the fields. Summer was nearly over.

Jumbo felt desperation surging inside him. There was still another two weeks before Mr. Bennet returned, and already they had collected more than twenty-eight pounds in eleven cocoa tins. Jumbo felt that the challenge had gone out of it. He wished that they had only three pounds, and had to find the other forty-seven. That would have made life interesting.

He decided he would go to the graveyard and think. He put on a yellow shirt and red bow tie, and set off. As he turned into the High Street, which was still being maintained by Bert Stiggins and his gang, Jumbo sighed. Even Bert had become boring since the kidnapping episode. Jumbo had only to whistle a few bars of "Baa, baa, black sheep," and Bert would do anything he asked.

Mr. Jefferson came to the door of his shop and stopped Jumbo.

"How are things going?" he asked. He took a keen interest in the Reform Club, and engaged Mike to do his deliveries every week.

"All right," said Jumbo dolefully. "We've got more than half."

"I was going to have a word with you about that," said Mr. Jefferson. "If you ask me, Jumbo, you've just about milked the village dry." He shook his head.

"What do you mean?" asked Jumbo.

"Done everything that needs doing," explained Mr. Jefferson. "There's a limit to what needs doing in a little place like this, you know. I've racked my brains, and I can't think of any more jobs for you to do. There just aren't the jobs any more, Jumbo."

Jumbo began to feel that things were livening up. Here was a problem.

"That's true," he said thoughtfully. "What we really need is a scheme that will bring money in from people outside the village."

"Well, if you could manage it," said Mr. Jefferson

apologetically. "I thought I'd just mention it. I hope you don't mind?"

"Not at all, Mr. Jefferson," said Jumbo. "I can't quite see your point. Now I come to think of it, the job time-table for next week isn't so full as last week's. I shall have to think of a new idea, or we won't have the fifty pounds in time."

He spoke the words joyfully. The almost-forgotten words began to run through his head again, in a swift, heady rhythm: "I'm a great reformer and a leader of men. I'm a great reformer and a leader of men."

As he made his way to the graveyard, he felt almost as he had done that evening when he had heard the words for the first time, and gone rushing down to the barn with a head full of glory. There was an important deci-sion to be made, and he, Jumbo Spencer, was going to make it. The blood hammered in his ears. Jumbo Spencer was alight again.

Jumbo intended to put Shoredale on the map. He was surprised now that he hadn't thought of it before. It was Mr. Jefferson's remark that money must come from out-side the village that had given him the idea. That, and the fact that Shoredale had never looked quite so lovely as it did, now that Bert Stiggins and his henchmen were working so hard on it. Jumbo could hardly bear to think of it being tucked away off the main road behind the trees, with hardly anyone knowing that it even existed.

He made a list of its beauties and places of interest, and their number startled him. They were certainly worth half a crown to see, and possibly a tip, too. He made a few rapid calculations, and the decision was made. Jumbo Spencer was in the tourist industry.

It took several days to arrange. Jumbo had to go and ask Mr. Potter's permission to show visitors round the church. This being given, he then approached Miss Mogg to see if she would mind letting people see round her house. It was very old, the oldest in the village, and had very low ceilings and bottle-glass windows. As an added attraction, from the kitchen rafters swung a cage containing a brightly-colored parrot who was rumored to be as old as Miss Mogg herself. Jumbo himself thought this unlikely. It certainly didn't look as old.

Miss Mogg was thrilled at the idea, and in any case she was eager to do anything for Jumbo to show her gratitude for the brand-new zebra crossing that now led from her very door right across to the post office. She made the journey several times a day, carefully keeping inside the black and white lines. It had changed her whole life.

Mike, who was very handy, was commissioned to build a gallows. He did this very realistically out of extremely ancient wood from a derelict cowshed, and a noose was constructed out of a tattered rope that looked at least several centuries old, and probably was, as it had been in Jumbo's loft for as long as he could remember. He also found some rusty chain, which was draped round the gallows as a final gruesome touch.

He did not think it would be fair to pass this off as an original, however. Once visitors had got over the initial shock of seeing the gallows, he intended to explain that this was only a replica, to give atmosphere to the village.

There was a good deal of publicity to attend to. Placards had to be put up, and Mike was kept busy with Olde English lettering. Bert Stiggins made his own signs saying "Keep off the grass and flower beds."

Jumbo made an arrangement with his mother that farmhouse teas should be served on card tables in the orchard, on condition that Maggots and two of her friends undertook all the arrangements, including the washing up.

"Mum," said Jumbo, "what did people used to wear in those days?"

"Which days, dear?" asked his mother vaguely.

"Olden days, Mum," said Jumbo, equally vaguely.

"Oh, I don't know, dear. All sorts of things."

This information was not much to go on. At the dress rehearsal for the next day, Maggots and her two friends were wearing dirndl skirts borrowed from their mothers. They came right down to their feet, and in fact were so long that Jumbo felt they were a positive danger to the farmhouse teas, and advised the girls to "hitch them up." They also wore aprons, mobcaps, and silk kerchiefs, and looked like colorful, tropical birds flitting among the low boughs of the orchard.

Mike was to wear a Robin Hood outfit he had been given for his birthday several years before and had considerably outgrown. The trousers barely came below his knees and the hat sat on his tufty hair at a decidedly rakish angle. Carrying out the same theme, Freckles had made himself a Friar Tuck outfit from sacking. He looked a cross between a monk and a corporation dustman, except with his hood on, when he immediately took on such a sinister aspect, that Jumbo decided that his job should be to stand beside the gallows and glare at people from the holes cut in the sacking for his eyes.

Jumbo himself, in the role of official guide, was to wear his gray suit, a white shirt and a tasteful dark red bow tie.

On the eve of the opening of Shoredale to the public as a place of historic interest, there was a frenzy of last-minute preparations. The postcards were arranged in boxes. These Jumbo was rather proud of. He had borrowed a camera and taken most of them himself. Others Freckles had taken, so that Jumbo himself could be on the pictures. Half of them had already been sold to villagers, and a further order had been placed with the chemist.

At dusk, Mike and Jumbo made a journey to the main road, carrying boards mysteriously swathed in newspaper. These they concealed in the ditch, and returned to Shoredale empty-handed.

By eight the next morning the whole village was astir. Maggots and company were setting up tables in the orchard, Jumbo was rehearsing his speech to an audience of thrushes in the tree outside his window, and everyone in Shoredale was polishing, cleaning, and scrubbing.

At half past nine Mike arrived at Jumbo's house. He

was wearing his Robin Hood outfit and carrying a bow and arrows so small that they were almost lost in his huge fists. He was wearing a pair of Wellington boots in an attempt to bridge the gap between his feet and where his breeches ended. Together he and Jumbo walked through the village and over the hill to the bus stop. There they took their boards from the ditch and uncovered them.

"You'd better put this on first," said Jumbo.

It was a sandwich board. On one side it said "Turn at the bus stop for the Ancient and Historic Village of Shoredale. Conducted Parties hourly. Church, thatch, beams, gallows, etc." On the other side it said "The Jumbo Spencer Reform Club invites you to visit Historic Shoredale."

Jumbo helped to pull it over Mike's head, then stepped back to admire the effect. It was certainly striking. Mike stood uncomfortably with his arms dangling. He took a few hesitant steps, but then seemed to find it more comfortable to stand still.

"I f-feel silly, Jumbo," he said.

"You're the best piece of publicity we've got, Mike," said Jumbo warmly.

This was certainly true. During the next few days many a motorist stopped and turned back after a brief glimpse of Mike's incredible figure, and wound his way up the lane to Shoredale in the hope of seeing others like him.

"Do I j-just stand here like this, Jumbo?" asked Mike. "All day?"

"You can walk up and down," said Jumbo. "Wave your arms about to attract attention when you see cars coming. And you could keep shooting arrows in the air. It will give you something to do to go after them. Yes, that's an idea. Try it, and see how it looks."

Obediently Mike fumbled with his minute bow and arrows, and finally succeeded in shooting an arrow a distance of about fifteen yards. He lumbered after it like an overgrown cupid.

"Very good," approved Jumbo. "Yes, do that, Mike. Now, just give me a hand with the signs, and I'll be off."

Together they put in position a newly painted sign-post which read "Ye Historic Village of Shoredale—½ mile" and which looked like any other signpost, except that it was five times as large.

Jumbo then set off back up the hill to the village. At the top he paused and looked round. He could see Mike's green figure busily shooting arrows in the air and chasing clumsily after them. He heard the hooting of a car, and nodded approval. A few minutes later he was overtaken by a car. Then another, and another. He quickened his step.

As he entered the High Street he could see a cluster of parked cars and a crowd of people waiting by the Pump, which was the starting point for the conducted tours. He decided not to hurry. It was only five to ten, and the parties did not start until the hour.

11

✷✷✷

JUMBO SPENCER–
OFFICIAL GUIDE

Freckles in his Friar Tuck outfit had taken charge of them and had obviously told them all about Jumbo, because they all turned and watched his approach with interest. Jumbo returned their gaze coolly. There were about fifteen people, half of them children.

"Good morning," said Jumbo, stepping on to the soapbox. "Welcome to the ancient and historic village of Shoredale. In a few minutes we will be starting on a conducted tour of its places of interest, including the ancient church, fifteenth-century cottages, village well, stocks and gallows. After this, light refreshments will be served in the orchard of White Walls Farm. Thank you."

He stepped down and set smartly off along the High Street in the direction of the church, followed by his flock. He kept up an almost continuous running commentary. He found that the words flowed like poetry in time to his steps. By the time they reached the church he was breathless.

The crowd "oo-ed" and "ah-ed" gratifyingly as he pointed out the features of interest. Mr. Potter, who had been standing in the porch listening, said "Good morning" to them and whispered, "Good work, Jumbo!"

All the way back a small boy who was dogging Jumbo's steps kept interrupting all his best soliloquies with "Where's the gallers? I wanna see the gallers!"

So Jumbo led them to the stocks and gallows. Freckles was there with his hood pulled over his eyes, looking like a medieval executioner, but the crowd were not so awed by him as they should have been, because they had seen the homely, freckled face and bright blue eyes that lay behind it. The little boy now made a sudden plunge forward and grabbed hold of the noose with the obvious intention of swinging on it.

His father stopped him just in time, and Jumbo breathed a sigh of relief. While he would gladly have hanged the child with his own hands, the gallows were not very safe and it would be a pity to lose them.

"What's them?" asked the boy, pointing to the stocks.

Jumbo told him, and mentioned the name of some well-known local criminals who had been imprisoned in them.

"I want to go in them," said the little boy.

"You be quiet," said his father.

"Not at all," said Jumbo, to whom an idea had just occurred.

He unlocked the padlock that held them down, put the boy's legs through and locked them again.

"You can stay here a bit if you behave yourself," said Jumbo severely. "Pretend you're Foxy Fred the Poultry Thief."

He turned to the crowd.

"The rest of us will go on to the fifteenth- and sixteenth-century cottages on our left," he said.

The boy's father seemed quite content to leave his son languishing in the stocks. As they entered Miss Mogg's dim little kitchen they could hear his exultant shouts:

"Come on, everybody, throw eggs at me! I'm Foxy Fred the Poultry Thief! Throw rotten eggs, throw tomatoes, throw anything!"

From time to time as they wandered through the low-ceilinged cottages, they could hear squeals of delight echoing from the top of the High Street. After ten minutes or so they emerged and went back to release him.

"Dad! Dad!" he cried as he saw them approaching. "Look at me!"

They looked, and Jumbo groaned with anguish. His hair and face were covered with slime and tomato pips. His hair was matted with egg yolk, and it was running in rich yellow streams down the front of his white shirt.

"Dad! Dad! They threw things at me!" he cried ecstatically.

Jumbo looked swiftly round. There was no sign of Freckles. Bert Stiggins and his gang, who had been hanging round the grass verges and flower beds in case anyone wanted to tip them, had disappeared. He turned to the boy's father.

"If you bring him up to our farm, my mother will clean him up," he offered. "And the rest of you can have refreshments."

So they released the boy and went up to the farm, where Maggots, waiting hopefully by the gate, squealed with delight at the sight of so many customers, and raced off to warn the others.

Jumbo's mother cleaned up Foxy Fred as best she could, and Jumbo escorted the party back to the Pump, where Freckles was waiting with the collection boxes. As the last car drew off Jumbo began to count the money. Counting tips and the refreshment money Maggots had taken, as well as the price of the tour, there was £2 1s. 3d. Jumbo was dazed. He had hardly recovered from his shock when more cars began to arrive. He took round two more parties before dinner and then went home, leaving a notice on the Pump saying "Gone to dinner. Next tour 2 pm."

By five o'clock Jumbo had taken round six parties and was exhausted. He was about to put a notice on the Pump saying "Closed for today," when a car purred up into the village. It was a strawberry pink Cadillac with enormous lashings of silver chrome and it reminded Jumbo of a swordfish. At the wheel was a crew-cut gentleman wearing dark sunglasses and a blue silk shirt.

"Say, kid," drawled the driver, "is this the ancient and historic village of Shoredale?"

"Yes, it is," said Jumbo.

"Fine," said the man who was obviously an American. "When's the next tour?"

"There aren't any more today," said Jumbo.

The man's face fell.

"Well, now, isn't that a shame!" he exclaimed. "I would just have loved to have seen around."

Jumbo took the American solo for the full tour. He had recognized the American as Red Macpherson, the film star. They had tea with Miss Mogg, who almost swooned with delight, and Red signed a photo of Jumbo and the gallows "For my little pal Jumbo in memory of our friendship," which gave the pleasing impression they had known each other for years.

Then Jumbo escorted Red to his car, which was surrounded by about thirty children. The film star pressed a note into Jumbo's hand and got in. Jumbo gave him a final wave as the swordfish leapt round the bend, and then looked down at the note in his hand. It was a five-pound note.

Jumbo wondered whether Red would have given it to him if he had known that he was about to drive into London with a notice stuck on the back of his strawberry pink Cadillac saying "Jumbo Spencer invites you to visit Historic Shoredale. Watch out for Robin Hood, then turn right."

Better go home and get some sleep, thought Jumbo. There'll be a rush on tomorrow.

"Jumbo!"

A voice cut through the dream Jumbo was having about being President of the United States and driving round in a strawberry pink Cadillac with a parrot perched on his shoulder.

"Jumbo!"

He sat up.

"Warrisit?" he asked. His mother was standing by his bed.

"Jumbo, get up. There's a man to see you."

"What sort of man?" demanded Jumbo, fencing for time.

"Don't be silly, dear. A man in a tweed coat. He says he's something to do with television. He looks familiar to me."

"Television?" Jumbo was halfway into his trousers. "Keep him talking, Mum, I'll be down in a minute."

He put on the red bow tie, ran the comb hastily through his hair, raced to the door of his room, and then walked very slowly and casually into the kitchen.

"Ah, so this is the young man."

Jumbo recognized John Macdonald, who interviewed people on the magazine program after the news. They shook hands.

"Glad to meet you," said Mr. Macdonald. "I've heard a lot about you. Look, you just get on with your breakfast and we'll talk while you're eating."

"I can't spare very long," said Jumbo, hoping his voice

wasn't trembling. "I've got a conducted tour on at nine o'clock."

"Ah, have you?" Mr. Macdonald sounded interested. "That just suits me fine. We want to start filming early while the light's good."

"Filming?" said Jumbo. The piece of ham he had in his mouth refused to go down. He tried to swallow and failed.

"Yes. We want to do some filming in the village, interview villagers, get the facts on this Reform Club of yours and so on. Then we'd like you to come up to London with us to appear in person on the program tomorrow night after we've shown the film."

Jumbo munched steadily, concentrating on his ham.

"All right," he said at last.

"Good." Mr. Macdonald got up. "I'll just tell the boys to get the cameras set up. Down by the Pump is your starting point, isn't it?"

He went to the door. In the farmyard Jumbo could see two large vans.

"All right, Dick!" shouted Mr. Macdonald. "Ready to start 0900 hours by the Pump. I'll be with you in a few minutes."

Jumbo suddenly remembered something.

"I shall have to be back by the day after tomorrow," he said.

"That can be arranged," said Mr. Macdonald. "That's your deadline, isn't it?"

Jumbo nodded.

"I've got to meet Mr. Bennet at eleven o'clock with the money," he said. "I'll see you down by the Pump."

All the time he was changing and all the way down to the village, he kept saying over and over again, "I'm a great reformer and a leader of men."

It was a great strengthener in times of crisis.

12

✠✠✠

JUMBO ON

TELEVISION

The village was in a turmoil. Despite Mr. Macdonald's request that everything should be kept as normal as possible, everybody seemed to have dressed up in their best things and kept inventing excuses to walk across the High Street in front of the cameras.

Before the conducted tour started they filmed an interview with Miss Mogg, who with tears in her eyes told them about the zebra crossing and walked across it wearing her best lace shawl to show them how safe it was.

It was dinner-time before they finished filming the conducted tour. The visitors, in their excitement at the prospect of appearing on television the next day, tipped heavily, and three cocoa tins were filled with their contributions.

After dinner the camera crew went down to the main road and took several shots of Mike in his Robin Hood outfit still shooting arrows into the air. John Macdonald then held a microphone in front of him and asked him for his comments on the Jumbo Spencer Reform Club.

Mike thought desperately, racking his brains for something to say. Then, like a flash, he remembered what Jumbo had told him to say right at the beginning of the holidays.

"N-n-n-no c-c-c-comment!" he stammered, and backed heavily away.

Then Jumbo insisted on taking them to the graveyard where the idea of the Jumbo Spencer Tourist Agency had been born.

"Do an interview with Mr. Potter," he said generously. "He does reforming as well. He could do with some publicity."

They made an early start to London the next day. Mrs. Spencer wanted to accompany them, but Jumbo persuaded her not to, feeling that this would look unmanly.

The whole village gathered to see them off. Freckles managed to fix a publicity poster on to the back of the vans, and then they were off amidst a burst of cheers and applause.

Jumbo spent all day at the television studios. He was taken to watch the film of Shoredale being cut and edited, and had lunch in the canteen with six famous people. After lunch he was put in a room with several easy chairs and some comics, while he waited for his turn to rehearse.

He couldn't settle down to reading. He kept thinking about Shoredale, and wondering what Maggots, Mike, and Freckles were doing. He hoped that Mike had remembered that Jumbo was away, and was not still shooting arrows into the air on the main road. They must be feeling very lost without him. After all, he was their leader.

He thought how hard they had worked during the last few weeks. He remembered how Maggots had trotted uncomplainingly backwards and forwards across the orchard from the farmhouse with trays of cakes and lemonade. He remembered how Freckles had spent whole hours cleaning windows and mending fences, and how Mike had sat up late into the night painting posters and making placards in his painstaking Olde English lettering.

He got up and opened the door. The corridor was empty, but he could hear voices from behind one of the doors farther down. He knocked softly.

The door opened, and there was Richard Fairfax, who introduced the program in which Jumbo was to appear.

"Hallo, son," he said. "We're not quite ready for you yet."

"I know," said Jumbo miserably. "I want to ask you something."

He told Mr. Fairfax about how Mike, Freckles, and Maggots had helped him with his scheme.

"And I want them to be on television as well," he said.

Mr. Fairfax consulted his watch.

"I wonder if we could make it," he said thoughtfully. "It's four hours before we're on the air."

"I don't think I want to be on television if they're not," said Jumbo.

"Wait a minute, I'll see what I can do."

Mr. Fairfax disappeared and Jumbo waited patiently in the corridor. After several minutes the door opened.

"They're coming," said Mr. Fairfax. "We shan't have time to rehearse them, but it won't matter. Now, if you'll just go back and wait a few more minutes, we'll be ready for you."

Jumbo went back to the lounge, feeling that he had just won one of the greatest victories of his career.

At six o'clock he was taken into the makeup room where a girl in a pink overall was waiting for him, and he was put in a dentist's chair with a cape round his neck.

Jumbo thoroughly enjoyed being made up. By the time the girl had finished he looked quite sunburned, like an explorer just back from the jungle. He looked at himself critically in the mirror. He thought he looked just a little youthful for a social reformer and leader of men. He ought to look more severe.

"Could you just try thickening up my eyebrows a bit?" he asked the girl.

She obligingly pencilled him in a pair of forbidding-looking eyebrows.

"That's better," said Jumbo approvingly.

At that moment Maggots, Freckles, and Mike came in,

and Jumbo supervised their makeup, too. They were all wearing their special costumes.

"There's no need to do my face," Freckles told the girl. "I'm wearing my hood down." He pulled it down over his eyes to show her.

"Oh, Freckles, you mustn't!" cried Maggots. "Your mother said you were to smile at her, and how can you with your hood down?"

So Freckles, too, was creamed and powdered.

They were led down a long, polished corridor to the large studio where Jumbo had rehearsed that afternoon. There they sat down in a corner, watching the monitor sets until their film came on.

"Good night, Miss Jones, and thank you," Richard Fairfax was saying. "And now, we are going to show you a film of a small country village. Very quiet, you might think, and not very interesting. But this is Shoredale. Look at this!"

Jumbo felt his throat tightening as the screen went blank for a moment, and then the familiar scene of the High Street, with its rusty Pump and neatly-trimmed verges and trees, and even Mr. Jefferson leaning at the door of his shop, came on to the screen. He watched spellbound. Shoredale was on the map, and he, Jumbo Spencer, had put it there.

Mr. Bennet went into the lounge of the London hotel where he had booked for the last night of his holiday.

He had been travelling for nearly twenty-four hours, and was tired. There was no one else in the lounge, so he switched on the television and then stretched wearily in one of the deep, plush armchairs. He closed his eyes while the set hummed and flickered, warming up.

". . . but this is Shoredale. Look at this!"

Mr. Bennet sat up with a jerk and opened his eyes. There was the High Street, the Pump, and surely that was Mr. Jefferson?

"This is Shoredale," said the commentator's voice, "home of Jumbo Spencer."

Jumbo Spencer! So that was it. Mr. Bennet leaned forward and listened intently while John Macdonald explained how Jumbo had started the Reform Club, how he had won a zebra crossing for his village, and how Mr. Bennet, the famous writer and philosopher, had promised to give Shoredale a village hall and playing-fields if Jumbo could earn fifty pounds in a month by his own efforts.

Mr. Jefferson and Miss Mogg smiled at him from the screen. Then the scene changed, and there was Jumbo Spencer himself, standing by the village Pump and surrounded by people.

He listened incredulously as the interviewer explained Jumbo's scheme for raising funds for the Reform Club and at the same time putting Shoredale on the map.

"Already the funds amount to well over a hundred pounds," he said, "and this is the last day that Shoredale

will be open to the public as a historic village. Let's go
with Jumbo Spencer as he conducts his last party round
the village."

There were shots of the church, of Miss Mogg's
kitchen and the swinging parrot, of Freckles, looking
like a member of the Ku Klux Klan standing by the gallows, and even of the village well.

"Is it a wishing-well?" asked a woman in the party,
peering over.

"Well, there's never any harm in trying," said Jumbo
judiciously, and Mr. Bennet was still chuckling when the
next scene flashed on.

"And this," Jumbo was saying, "is Shoreham Manor,
historic house of the famous writer and philosopher,
William Bennet, who is at present abroad. Unfortunately, I can't show you the interior, though it is very
nice, with lots of books and pictures, but you can walk
up the drive and look at the outside."

Mr. Bennet could not help wondering where Briggs
had been while all this was taking place. He was not to
know that Jumbo had sent Bert Stiggins and his gang to
raid the orchard and act as a decoy while the filming was
taking place.

The film ended with shots of Mike shooting arrows on
the main road, and finally of the site where Jumbo hoped
the village hall would eventually stand.

"With us in the studio tonight," said Richard Fairfax,
"is Jumbo Spencer, with three of the members of his

club whom you have already seen in the film, Maggots, Mike, and Freckles."

The camera swung round for a close-up of the three, and at the sight of them Mr. Bennet's laughter broke out uncontrollably. A waiter, happening to come to the door and look in, was so startled that he hurried down to the offices to tell the manager that the writer chap in Number 37 had gone mad. Mr. Bennet finally wiped his eyes and tried to concentrate on what Jumbo was saying.

"And this is only the beginning," Jumbo was saying.

"I would like to see a village hall and playing-fields in every single village in this country." (Mr. Bennet hoped that he would not be expected to pay for them all.)

"I would like to see white pavilions, even the roof would be white, with a veranda and deck-chairs so that everyone can come and watch. Just think, no one would ever be bored again."

"That, then, is what you are trying to stamp out, is it, Jumbo?" asked Richard Fairfax. "Boredom?"

"Definitely," said Jumbo. "There's nothing worse. And I'd just like to end by thanking Mr. Bennet for his kindness in offering to give the village a hall and playing-fields. I think it will make him very happy and he'll never regret it."

"Thank you very much, Jumbo Spencer. And now, is there anything the other three members of the club wish to say before we leave them?" asked Richard Fairfax.

The cameras turned on the other three.

"Hello, Mum," said Freckles.

There was a close-up of Maggots. She hung her head and smiled and the cameras moved on to Mike. He seemed to be groping for words. His lips twitched, but no sound came. Then, at last, with a tremendous effort he spoke:

"N-n-n-n-no c-c-c-c-c-comment!" he said.

13

THE END OF
IT ALL

Jumbo opened his eyes. The September sunlight was
flooding the room and the orchard was full of whistling
birds. He sat up and looked out over the familiar fields to
the far woods, and sighed with contentment. Today he
would go to see Mr. Bennet and the bargain would be
sealed. His work was done. He felt a little sad at the
thought. With its village hall and playing-fields and
gleaming white pavilion, Shoredale would be a perfect
village, and perfection was a little boring.

This morning as he put on his bow tie he eyed it rather
dubiously. He was not at all sure that it was not becoming a little boring wearing one every day. He went down
to breakfast.

"Is that you, Jumbo?" called his mother.

"Yes, Mother," said Jumbo patiently. "It's me."

"I wasn't going to wake you till later," she said. "You had such a late night."

"The birds woke me," said Jumbo. "Besides, I've got an important appointment at eleven."

At half past ten he set out down the High Street carefully wheeling a very heavy wheelbarrow. People called out to him as he passed. Mr. Jefferson came out of his shop.

"Very nice show on the television last night," he said. "I thought they did us proud."

"You came out very well, Mr. Jefferson," said Jumbo.

"Do you think so?" said Mr. Jefferson, grinning hugely. "You weren't so bad yourself, young Spencer. Wish my boy had as much initiative as you."

Jumbo did not think it tactful to remind Mr. Jefferson that at one time he would not allow his son to play with Jumbo because he was a "bad influence." He merely smiled and carried on. Miss Mogg was carefully making her way over her zebra crossing and she, too, smiled and waved. Jumbo felt glad to be a leader of men.

In the graveyard the leaves were beginning to drift into glowing piles against the gray tombstones, lit into fire by the shafts of sun that streamed between the trees. He walked slowly up the drive to Shoreham Manor until he came face to face once more with the brass knocker.

"Oh, it's you, young Spencer. Mr. Bennet's expecting you." Briggs seemed more genial than usual this morning.

He showed Jumbo into the library and left him alone. Again Jumbo was awed by the stillness of the room and the strange certainty that those hushed volumes were aware of him as they leaned up there in their dusty silences. The picture still hung above the mantelpiece, and Jumbo, looking at it again, became absorbed in its triangles and squares. Again he was surprised by Mr. Bennet.

"Still like it?"

Jumbo turned round.

"Yes, sir. Good morning, sir. I hope you enjoyed your holiday?"

"Very much," said Mr. Bennet. "Did you?"

This morning he was wearing a Chinese brocade smoking jacket of splendid dyes, and Jumbo was so absorbed in admiration of it that he was taken somewhat off balance, and could only murmur, "Yes, thanks," in reply.

"Now let's get down to business," said Mr. Bennet. "Have you got the money?"

"Yes, sir," said Jumbo.

"Where?"

"Outside," said Jumbo.

"Outside!" cried Mr. Bennet incredulously. "What on earth . . . ? You'd better bring it in this minute."

"But, sir," protested Jumbo, "it's ——"

"Bring it in," ordered Mr. Bennet.

Jumbo went out and came back, an agitated Briggs at his side, wheeling the wheelbarrow over the parquet floor.

"What on earth?" expostulated Mr. Bennet. As far as he could see it was a load of old tins.

"I tried to tell you," said Jumbo. "The money's all in tins!"

Mr. Bennet sat down rather suddenly.

"How much is there?" he asked.

"A hundred and three pounds four shillings and nine-pence," said Jumbo.

"So the bargain is sealed," said Mr. Bennet. "I give you the hall and playing-fields."

"And pavilion, sir," added Jumbo respectfully.

"And pavilion," agreed Mr. Bennet. "The question is, what are you going to do with the rest?"

"The rest of what, sir?" asked Jumbo, puzzled.

"The rest of this," said Mr. Bennet, indicating the cocoa tins with a wave of his hand. "I only asked for fifty pounds, you know. A bargain's a bargain. You must find some other use for the rest."

"Oh thank you, sir," cried Jumbo, "I will!"

"Well, good-bye, Jumbo," said Mr. Bennet. They shook hands. Jumbo felt they understood one another.

"I almost forgot," said Jumbo. "Mr. Potter said would you call to see him at four o'clock?"

"Yes," said Mr. Bennet. "Yes, I can manage that. Good-bye, Jumbo, for the present."

As he went back through the churchyard Jumbo's eye settled on a notice-board that had stood there for several years. It was the first time he had really looked at it and thought what it meant. A slow smile spread over his face. A decision had been made.

After dinner Jumbo's mother asked him to sort the

apples, pack them in tissue paper, and store them in the attic. He was glad of something to do. All the excitement of the previous weeks had left him with a curious sense of anti-climax. He sat in the dusty backwater of the attic, mechanically polished the pale green apples, his eyes fixed in thought.

"Jumbo!" he heard his mother's voice floating up. "Jumbo! Come down, will you? I want you."

His mother was in the kitchen. He noticed she was wearing her best blue silk dress, and wondered why.

"Jumbo, just run down to Miss Mogg with this recipe, will you?" she said. "I promised I'd let her have it this afternoon."

"Before tea?" asked Jumbo.

"Yes, if you don't mind, dear. It's only a quarter past four."

Jumbo took the recipe and went out. He kicked at stones along the road as he went. He turned the corner into the High Street with his head bent and eyes on the road. A great roar went up. Amazed, he lifted his head. The whole street seemed to be full of people, and they were singing. "For he's a jolly good fellow, for he's a jolly good fellow," they roared.

Jumbo felt an electric shiver run up his spine and out at the roots of his hair. The old magic was at work. He advanced, his head held proudly, a lump in his throat, and his heart beating with unbearable excitement.

He saw that long tables on trestles had been set out. They were covered with white cloths and great vases of flowers, great shaggy chrysanthemums and brilliant dahlias. Hardly an inch of cloth could be seen between the piles of food that were spread out. It seemed endless. It seemed to stretch the whole length of the village street.

Jumbo became aware that they had stopped singing and were cheering and shouting, and that Mr. Potter had put his hand on his shoulder and was leading him to the head of the table. Jumbo looked up and through a blur saw the faces of his friends swimming in a mist. As it cleared he

picked out Freckles, grinning widely, Mike, his face alight, and Maggots, half-choking with pride and pleasure.

Farther down he could see old Miss Mogg wearing her lavender shawl and nodding happily, and even Bert Stiggins was waving one hand while he fumbled for a tomato sandwich with the other. Right at the far end, facing Jumbo himself, sat Mr. Bennet. He raised his hand in greeting and Jumbo acknowledged his salute.

Mr. Potter raised his hand for silence and in a moment the noise stopped. The street was silent but for the whistling of birds in the cottage gardens.

"Jumbo Spencer," he said, "Shoredale is proud of you. We are grateful to Mr. Bennet, who has showed such kindness in giving us our hall and playing-fields, and we are grateful to every single person who has done anything to help this wonderful scheme. But most of all, Jumbo, we are grateful to you. Because without you there would have been no scheme at all, and—well, Jumbo, because you are our leader!" he finished and sat down.

There was a deafening roar of applause. It rang in Jumbo's ears and made him dizzy. Again the green boughs rocked into a spinning blur. Then all at once it was quiet. Jumbo looked down the long line of faces turned expectantly towards him. He suddenly felt small and humble.

"Thank you," he said. His voice hardly came out at all.

He cleared his throat and tried again.

"Thank you," he said again, more loudly. After all, they obviously expected a speech. He felt his brain beginning to clear.

"This is a day I shall never forget," he went on. "Today we have won a great reform for the village of Shoredale. We are to have our own hall, with blue velvet curtains and footlights, a playing-field with cricket pitch and tennis courts, and a pavilion painted all white, including the roof, with a veranda and deck-chairs for everyone to sit on. And before I end, I would like to say that Mr. Bennet will only take fifty pounds from the Reform Club Fund. That leaves fifty-three pounds four shillings and ninepence. He said I was to find some other use for it."

A murmur ran through the crowd and people turned to look at Mr. Bennet.

"I'm not the only reformer in this village, you know," said Jumbo. "Mr. Potter is one as well. And I've decided to give him the money for the Church Restoration Fund."

Cheering broke out again and Jumbo sat down abruptly. He felt that he had had about as much as he could stand. He was vaguely aware that Mr. Potter had stood up and was making a speech of thanks, but all the while his eyes were fixed on a ham roll that stood temptingly within a few inches of his hand. Mr. Potter sat down, and Jumbo reached for the roll.

It was growing dusk and the air was cooling when the

tables were finally cleared and the trestle tables taken down and stacked against the walls. Most of the villagers drifted away to their own homes, or stood talking quietly in groups.

Jumbo walked slowly back up the High Street. The air was full of the sharp fragrance of autumn, of bonfire smoke and damp earth. He wondered how he could spend the last few days of the holiday. He intended to do something really destructive. He was tired of being the "golden boy" of the village. He wanted people to be suspicious of him again, and be referred to as "that Jumbo Spencer!" His mind spilled with black schemes. One of them was to string Bert Stiggins by the waist from the gallows, but he reflected that the gallows would hardly stand the strain. He could set fire to Bert Stiggins's shed, but it might be better to wait for a really dry spell.

"Off home now, Jumbo?" It was Mr. Bennet.

"Yes, sir."

"Are you satisfied now?" asked Mr. Bennet, regarding Jumbo almost fiercely from under his bushy brows.

"I think so," said Jumbo slowly. "I'm very grateful, we all are, and glad that we're going to have a hall. But things seem a bit boring now, with nothing left to fight for."

"There's always something left to fight for," said Mr. Bennet. "I'm a lot older than you, and I've never been short of something. You'll find something, Jumbo."

That he felt certain of.